I0619159

EARTH ENDURES

BLEAK

JACQUELINE DRUGA

VULPINE

PRESS

Copyright © Jacqueline Druga 2019

All rights reserved. No part of this publication may be reproduced, stored in or introduced into a retrieval system or transmitted in any form or by any means, electronic, mechanical, photocopying, recording or otherwise without prior written permission from the publisher.

This novel is a work of fiction. Names, characters, places and incidents are either the product of the author's imagination or are used fictitiously, and any resemblance to any person or persons, living or dead, is entirely coincidental. No affiliation is implied or intended to any organisation or recognisable body mentioned within.

Published by Vulpine Press in the United Kingdom in 2019

Cover by Claire Wood

ISBN: 978-1-83919-280-7

www.vulpine-press.com

For my son, Noah, my sounding board and reality checker.
You truly are my muse.

PART ONE: THE PLAN

ONE

A single tap of hail hit against the windshield, but Reyanne Harper dismissed it as one of those pesky pieces of gravel. After all, it was spring and the dreaded road construction season had begun. She didn't think much about it, why would she? She heard it and dismissed the sound. It was still early and she just wanted to get to Grinds for a latte and one of those egg white bites, if they had any left. They seemed to always run out before nine.

So far it was turning into a great day; great days for her were few and far between. Despite the fact that she'd had very little sleep, Rey was still up before her alarm clock went off. She'd even had time to put on a little makeup. Her students at Saint Germaine would surely comment. They always did when she did her hair and makeup. Plus, Rey wasn't running late and that was an oddity in itself.

She'd not only be there before first bell, at her current travel rate, even with stopping for coffee, she'd be there before the first bus arrived.

Perhaps she'd even get a latte for Mr. Hibbs, the poor unfortunate teacher on bus-greeting duty. Which meant he had to be there an hour earlier.

The sun was shining with only a few clouds in the sky, the temperature was perfect, and she got what she considered 'Princess Parking' in the lot by the coffee shop.

All that positivity changed in an instant when the sky quickly clouded over and the bright blue sky turned gray and threatening.

Thinking *Wow that was fast*, Rey turned off her car and stepped out. One clap of thunder and it began.

Tiny particles of hail began sounding like a thick rain as they hit against the ground. Rey was only fifty feet or so from the entrance, but before she even made it to the door, the hail went from peaceful sounding drops to menacing *thunks*.

The tiny ice transformed from cereal size to golf ball size, and by the time she hurried inside freakishly huge chunks of ice rained down, some the size of basketballs. They fell fast and ferociously.

Like the others that stood beside her watching out the window, Rey cringed and jolted, often afraid to look when she saw people running to get into their cars or take cover.

Hail landed on cars, smashing roofs and breaking windshields, alarms rang out with screams from people pelted by the heavy objects, some falling down unconscious when they were hit. Vehicles on the road swerved and crashed; it was nothing less than a wall of broken ice pouring down from above. Even though there was an entire floor between her and the roof of the coffee shop, she could still hear the hail crashing through.

Her lucky day feeling and being early for work was suddenly gone.

Rey would be stuck in the coffee shop until the cars on the road were moved. Thankfully, for her job's sake, she knew school would be delayed too.

That happened a lot.

For all the emotions Rey felt while watching the freak storm—fearful, saddened—one thing Rey didn't feel … shocked.

It didn't surprise her one bit. It was the third of such storms in just over two weeks. It was par for the course with everything else that was happening.

No one was really prepared, but there was nothing they could do about it. The hail storm was one of many things that had happened and would continue to happen. All the greatest minds in the world concurred this weather was the onset of the next extinction-level event. One that would take hundreds of years to complete.

It was only the beginning. Rey was just happy she wouldn't be around to see it all come to an end. At least that was what she believed.

When he was sixteen years old, Colonel Aldar Finch was arrested for the fifth time. Nothing major, or violent. Various forms of shoplifting, all of which involved food. It wasn't that he was hungry, but his family was. His mother would never admit she didn't have enough to eat. That wasn't her style. She was a strong, proud black woman, who worked two jobs to support her two kids after her husband died.

Aldar was twelve when his father passed away; his little sister Mariam was only three. His mother worked full time as a receptionist at the blood bank, and on weekends she worked at the hotel as a desk clerk.

Despite working so much, money was always tight. It was expensive raising two children, and his mother never asked for a handout, never received welfare. Only occasionally would she go to the church's foodbank, and that killed her. Aldar saw it on her face. If there was never enough on the table, she wouldn't admit it, she would just say she wasn't hungry.

She was too proud.

That was when Aldar decided to step in.

He wanted to get a job, he really did, but he was the one who babysat when his mother worked. Plus, he was young and no one wanted to hire him.

So he lied. He lied to his mother about doing odd jobs. Jobs that paid for the extra food she would discover when she got home, or the takeout pizza and hamburgers.

Aldar was good at what he did. He wasn't proud of it, but he justified his actions. Plus, he committed far more crimes than he was ever caught for.

His mother never condoned what he did, and when the police would bring him home or call her, she was furious. She laid into him, punished him, cried at the thought of her own failures.

It wasn't her failure, Aldar tried to make her see. She was a good woman, he loved her, he just hated to see his mother so upset when they didn't have enough money to get a full order of groceries. While other kids bought lunch in school, or packed amazing deli choices, they went to school with jelly sandwiches, leftovers in foil, or premade ramen noodles, which were tacky, and would be in clumps by the time lunch rolled around.

Until Aldar started creatively thieving food, they never

had takeout.

He knew the Pizza Palace delivery guy would take more than one order with him on his route and never locked his car when he went to knock on the door.

People were creatures of habit. The same people would order on the same night. Aldar would follow the delivery driver and snatch up one of those unattended pizzas. Something he would do only once a month.

Other times for food, he'd hit the grocery store.

Aldar wasn't a bad kid. He never said a mean word, didn't fight, went to school and got good grades. He just … took things for the benefit of his family.

The first two times he was busted, they let him go. Didn't even tell his mother. Third and fourth time, he was taken into the police station, charges were pressed, and the judge made him work at Rainbow Kitchen, the church-run soup kitchen, for three Sundays. The fifth and final time, the fine was more than his mother could pay, and when Aldar came home from school the day after his hearing, he was shocked to see a military man in his living room.

"Aldar." His mother, still wearing her blood bank uniform, stood from the couch the second he walked into the apartment. "This is Staff Sergeant Gimble, he's with the air force. I work with his wife at the blood bank."

"Son," the sergeant said, extending his hand. "Your mother tells me you may be in need of direction."

Sergeant Gimble wasn't just some random co-worker's husband offering to be a father figure, he was a recruiter.

Back then, Aldar, in all his naivety, believed his mother had already signed up to send him off to the army, or one of those other branches of the service.

To appease his mother, Aldar listened to him. He didn't know if Gimble had some special secret brainwashing technique, but before he knew it, he was downtown at the federal building taking the aptitude test. However, the moment he found out that he scored exceptionally high, and he could pretty much have his pick of careers, Aldar was quick to say, "I wanna fly jets."

The rest was history.

He never would have imagined his drive to succeed in the air force, or how much he would love it. It not only got him off the streets and out of the neighborhood, it got his mother and sister out as well.

He kept enough out of his pay for spending money and sent the rest to his mother. The longer he was in the more he made, and he tried to give back as much as he could. He paid back the pizza shop, the corner store, and donated his time when he could to helping troubled teens.

He was raised by a good woman and he was a good man. He never married, not that he didn't want to or didn't try. Three times he was engaged and they all broke it off, hating to compete with his job. His job became a bigger issue when he was accepted by NASA and the Space Corps program.

He manned dozens of space flights and was essential in the development and testing of the Omni, which was in a sense the nearest thing to a starship, though not quite as big or futuristic as movies would depict them.

Technology had advanced since the days of the shuttle, and Aldar was right there with it. He was a pioneer in the Space Corps, which was in its infancy when he joined.

He wanted to fly jets ... that he did.

Aldar also made two other predictions in his life, that he would become president and would save the world.

The presidency dropped off his radar of ambitions and 'saving the world' was more of a joke. Until the day he was asked to do so.

Not so much save the world but to be instrumental in saving humanity.

Aldar humbly accepted the request.

His days and nights were consumed with training and learning all that he could for the mission. It included frequent meetings and planning sessions.

Aldar didn't mind those; they were all crucial in building a successful mission. And for the sake of the world they had to be successful.

Like always, he was one of the first to arrive. Second only to General Hank Lang who stood outside the meeting building smoking a cigarette.

He was the same age as Aldar, he'd just made it up the ladder a lot faster.

"General." Aldar saluted when he approached.

"Al." The general shook his hand.

"Thought you'd quit smoking," Aldar said.

"I did. I missed it, used to love it. Still do. But ... in light of recent events ..." He shrugged and hit his cigarette. "What do I have to lose, right?'

"You have a point. Anyone else here?"

"Nope. Just us. Dr. Gale's flight hasn't landed yet. We still have a half hour before the rest of the committee arrives.

You're early. Where's your partner in crime? I thought he'd come with you."

Aldar facially grimaced, while his insides churned at the thought of Captain Henning. He had flown with him many times, and Aldar was the first to disagree with the committee's choice of Henning for the mission. It was too important. While Henning had skills, he just, to Aldar, was unrefined. There weren't many people that Aldar didn't like ... unfortunately, Henning was one of them.

Techno dance music blasted as if it were some sort of party, rather than a photo shoot. But that was just the style of Miles the photographer. Even when a shoot went along with a serious story, he tried to lighten the mood. It just so happened that his current project was taking pictures of the year's Sexiest Man Alive. So he wanted things to feel upbeat and fun. Miles was the best of the best and was honored to be photographing Captain Curt 'The Clutch' Henning. He was a striking and fit young man, a hotshot pilot and astronaut, who gained the nickname 'The Clutch' because he had an uncanny streak of saving people and clutching them out of danger. Curt called it luck; he just happened to be in the right place at the right time. Which so happened to be any time danger struck.

People loved being around him. Not just for Curt's charm and humor, but they felt safe.

"If anything happens, hey, The Clutch is here."

"Come on, Clutch." A young female beckoned the tall and striking dark-haired astronaut. "One drink." She held up a glass to him.

"As much as I want to …" He winked. "I can't, ma'am," he said in his smooth country-boy way. "I have a real important meeting in about thirty minutes. Maybe less."

"People, people," Miles called out. "Can we get this back on track? I want to get the shot in front of the windows before I lose my lighting."

The studio was on the thirtieth floor. The windows were from floor to ceiling with a view of Houston like no other. The sky was perfectly blue and the sun was out of the shot.

He needed The Clutch and the two females to hurry along and get in front of the window. They could enjoy the craft services and drinks after.

The large studio was packed with assistants, agents, and catering people. All normal for a day on set.

Clutch moved to the window with the two models. He sipped on a bottle of water. "This is a heck of a view."

"I'm sure it's nothing compared to what you've seen up there," Miles said. "Clutch, could I get you to undo your shirt, please?"

"Sure." He shrugged, handing his water off to an assistant, and immediately undoing the buttons on his shirt. Just as he reached the final button a hum filled the air.

Miles heard and felt it. A vibration that caused a buzz, like a bug had entered his ear. As he registered what was about to unfold, vertigo set in. "Earthquake." Miles barely got the word out of his mouth before the floor began to shake.

As expected it caused a panic to those in the room. Not Miles though, he was accustomed to them. The mild quaking was nothing to worry about. In fact, Miles called out,

"Stay center of the room, stay calm. It's fine."

And it was, until the shaking grew violent and the roaring it produced became louder.

Suddenly, those trying to remain calm rushed for the elevators.

Were they insane? Miles thought and ran to stop them. "Just hold on to something," he shouted. "Don't run. Don't panic. Stay away from the elevators!"

Crash.

The first of the windows shattered, and Miles spun around to look. When he did, he watched the red-haired model sail out backwards, arms extended as if she were doing a backwards dive from a springboard.

The word "No!" crept up his chest, hit his throat, but before he could scream in horror The Clutch lived up to his name. It was almost like he had a keen sense it was going to happen. He reached out, grabbing the red-haired model's arm, grasping tight as she plunged out, and secured her just as she disappeared from Miles' sight.

Clutch was chest flush to the floor, holding on to her with one hand, and with the other he grasped the metal window frame as the building swayed, shook and the windows burst around him.

Miles was mesmerized, shocked that he had saved her. He knew he had to help, and he would, but first he did what any great photographer would do at that moment: he took a picture.

The high rise leaned so much, there was a feeling in Miles that it would fall over. It would survive another earthquake, especially this one.

He raced over to Clutch and, using that same metal frame that Clutch held, pressed his foot against it and grabbed on to Clutch's legs. He could see the model dangling, the look of terror on her face was immeasurable.

Holding on to those legs, Miles saw it through the corner of his eye, a rolling body. It was Anthony, one of his grips. Anthony rolled fast toward the window. He tried, Miles really tried to pull at Clutch. He reached out to grab him, but the momentum was too great and Anthony sailed out the window.

The earthquake stopped the second Anthony caught the air of his fall and his screams were heard as he fell to his death.

The ground may have stopped shaking, but Miles and everyone else knew, it wasn't over, not by a long shot.

TWO

Teaching was the one thing that gave Rey happiness in her life. But even that rarely made her smile. It kept her focused, a reason to get up. She dreaded summer vacation, which was a mere month away.

It never used to be that way.

At one point Rey had been full of life. How quickly all that changed when the weather changed. Rey used to joke years earlier that Pennsylvania was the East Coast equivalent of Washington state when it came to the weather. Bright and sunny, then muggy, then rainy for a few days ... repeat.

She had experienced flash floods in her lifetime, but nothing major. Until the great flash flood of her hometown of Canonsburg brought her into a reality she had only seen on the evening news.

The waters had rushed into town ten months earlier with the freak vengeance of a tsunami, then buried the town in four feet of mud. One hundred and twenty people lost their lives that night. Of those were her mother, father, husband, sister, and six-year-old niece. They were all having dinner that night at her parents' house when the storm blew in.

Rey would have been there and died as well, had she not been out with the faculty from school for a 'last day of school' outing twenty miles away.

That storm was the first harsh, disaster-level weather to blast the area, and since then it had become commonplace.

The only bright spot to her day was school, and lately, technically, it wasn't that bright.

Not five hours earlier, Rey was darting foot size hailstones, shivering; now she stood in her classroom, air conditioning blasting and she still sweat. It was so hot and humid, nothing helped. The air was thick, visibly thick. The particles that floated in it carried a red hue when they reflected the sun.

A facemask warning hadn't been issued, but Rey knew it wasn't far from happening.

Her fifth-grade classroom was dark so the twelve students could see the projection of images on the screen.

"Good one, good one," she said pleasantly. "Okay … how about this one?" She changed the image.

The classroom went silent, not a student raised their hand upon seeing the green leafy ball-looking object. "No one? Would you believe that"—she pointed to the picture—"is this." She reached down to her desk and lifted a clear plastic package that contained salad.

The class erupted in excited noises.

"How?" a student asked.

"See, you don't see these anymore. Heads of lettuce they were called. Iceberg. At one time people went into the stores and bought them," she explained. "You eat the bag of lettuce and don't think about it. Because you just don't know."

"What's the difference?" a student asked.

"Oh the head of lettuce tastes much better. Juicy and

fresh ... this is processed, packed, and slightly dried to pre-serve shelf life, to eliminate waste. Fifteen years ago, people wasted a lot of food. A lot. For example, the world used to produce forty million pounds of iceberg lettuce a year. Fifty percent of that was thrown out. Never eaten. Because of everything that's happening, we can't grow lettuce like we did, the weather isn't right for it. So instead of making people pay exuberant prices for a head that they will waste, they only are available in bags. Except in really expensive res-taurants."

A student raised her hand. "Will we not have it at all one day?"

"Sadly," Rey sighed out. "But ... you won't have to see that day. All the greatest minds are working right now, and that started with the building of—"

"Miss Harper." At the same time the school secretary, Nancy, called Rey's name she knocked once on the arch of the classroom door. Then she stepped in.

"Yes?"

"I'm going to watch your class. You're needed down at Mrs. Stone's office immediately."

"Everything okay?" Rey asked.

"Just go down."

Rey didn't hesitate. Immediately she worried. Did some-thing happen to her brother? Her nieces and nephews? It could have been anything, but one thing was for sure, it had to be an emergency. Ever since flood day, Rey always thought of the worst. She moved at a quick pace to the prin-cipal's office located on the same floor. When she stepped inside, Principal Stone was standing there in the office with two men. One was a general in full uniform, the other was a studious-looking man in a suit.

"Ms. Harper," Principal Stone said. "This is General Kiphflor and Mr. Tom Waite of NASA."

Their introduction caused Rey to step back in shock. "This is a surprise. Pleasure to meet you." She shook their hands. "I don't understand. What's going on?"

"Six years ago," Tom said, "educators across the country were invited to submit an essay to NASA and its partner Flagship of Humanity. It was an essay on how you feel you would save the world, or rather humanity. Do you recall?"

Rey partially shrugged. "That was six years ago. I remember submitting it. I vaguely remember what I wrote."

"One of the pivotal portions of that essay dealt with the Androski Wormhole," Tom said. "Does that ring a bell?"

"Ah, yes," Rey said, "some. Androski Wormhole Theory. Most of my essay, if I remember correctly, was really out there. Using the Androski Wormhole was one part."

"Out of the seventy-three thousand essays we received, yours was the only one that mentioned the Androski Wormhole," Tom said.

"Probably because it is really farfetched and not real."

Tom looked at the general then back to Rey. "As farfetched as it sounded, it is real. And because of that, amongst other truly remarkable and insightful things you had in that essay, you have been chosen."

"Oh my God," Rey squealed with excitement. "I won an essay contest? That's great. And you guys came all the way here to tell me?"

The general looked at her. "This isn't something that is easily said on the phone."

"Wow, my prize must be nice." Rey smiled. "I'm really honored."

"It exceeds any monetary value. We are the ones honored. Congratulations." Tom once again extended his hand to her. "You will be part of The Noah Project."

Mouth slightly agape, Rey slowly slid her hand from Tom's and titled her head with a dumbfounded look. "Excuse me?"

There was nothing like a middle-of-the-day candy, especially when the vending machine spewed out a bunch after the earthquake struck.

Aldar's favorite type was amongst the scattered bars on the floor. He grabbed one. He had planned on going to lunch after the meeting, but since the meeting was delayed, he needed something in his stomach. The quake was a decent size and he doubted any restaurants would even be open for the remainder of the day.

When he returned to the meeting room, he knew something was wrong. Everyone was on their phones. He would have thought that it was another awful event somewhere had they all not been smiling and whispering.

Eating the candy, Aldar walked back into the meeting room. Most of the committee was there, along with several tech people. Dr. Nathan Gale had arrived. Lucky for him his flight had landed just moments before the quake.

Gale always seemed nervous to Aldar, or on some sort of amped-up drug. He moved quickly, always shuffling

18

through papers with a lap top and a tablet in front of him. The average height, thinner man leaned on the nerdy side. To Aldar he seemed nice enough, though they'd only had a handful of conversations. All of them brief and all of them work related. The earth science guru made eye contact with Aldar. Aldar gave a nod of acknowledgement.

"Did you see?"

Aldar heard the question and turned his head to General Lang who was behind him.

"I'm sorry, sir?" Aldar asked.

"A good damn reason for holding us up?"

"The quake."

"Sort of, I mean this." The general chuckled, and like a peacock he extended his chest with pride as he showed Aldar the phone. "Did you see this?"

Aldar looked down to the image. It was of his co-pilot, Curt, holding onto the arm of a woman dangling and near death. Aldar grumbled a, "No. Didn't see that."

"Living up to his name again, I suppose."

"Henning?" Aldar played dumb.

"No, The Clutch."

"Yeah. I suppose."

"Makes us proud."

"Yes, much to be said about being the sexiest man alive honor."

"I'm talking about the heroism."

Aldar grumbled.

"You know." The general pulled his phone away. "I hear

that in your tone."

"What?"

"The resentment. The jealousy." He waved his finger. "Green is not your color."

"No, it is not. Which is why I joined the air force and not the army."

General Lang laughed. "Good one."

Both men turned when applause erupted in the room.

Curt walked in. He lifted his hand in a bashful way. "Thanks, but I was in the right place at the right time. Houston is the earthquake capital of the world, so I guess I'm always in the right place."

Laughter.

Someone said, "That's why they call you The Clutch."

Aldar grumbled which garnished a look from the general. He then took his seat at the table and Curt sat next to him.

A packaged cake was tossed in front of him.

"What's this?" Aldar asked.

"I swiped that for you from the photo shoot," Curt answered. "It is amazing. Has like a strawberry cream inside."

"Why in the world would you steal food for me?" Aldar asked.

"Just really good. They don't sell them anywhere."

"Thank you." Aldar examined the pastry and placed it down when a bound thin manuscript was placed before him.

"What my secretary is handing out," the general said, "is an essay."

"Essay?" Curt questioned softly as he flipped the pages. "I thought an essay was like two pages."

"This is very detailed," the general continued. "Six years ago we asked educators across the country to submit their ideas on how they would save humanity. Sometimes it takes more than the minds on the payroll."

Aldar briefly skimmed. "Sir." He raised his hand. "Was this your guide book?"

"Some, yes," he answered. "Some we had already started before we even read this. This teacher really worked hard on this essay, that was why she won."

"What exactly did she win?" Aldar asked.

"We wanted a representation of the general public on this mission. Someone relatable. And while everyone knows and trusts you two"—he pointed to Aldar and Curt—"not everyone can relate to being the sexiest man alive," he joked. "So, Ms. Harper will be arriving at the training and launch facility in West Virginia tomorrow. That's why Mission Specialist Vonn isn't here. He's there to greet her. I thought he'd be the best one."

"Wait. Wait," Curt whispered to Aldar. "We're putting an educator on this mission? NASA tried this once before and we all know how that turned out."

Aldar shot him a glare. "For real?"

"What? Too soon?"

Aldar shook his head and looked at the essay.

"How can it be too soon? It was decades ago."

"Stop," Aldar whispered a scold.

The general continued. "I want all of you to learn this essay, read it. She's a pretty smart individual."

Aldar would read it. He'd find time in the evening. If the woman was chosen to go, there had to be something pretty special about her manuscript. He looked at the first page, starting to read it until he heard the general announce Nate.

"Dr. Gale," the general called his name.

"Thank you." Nate stood at the end of the table. "I wanted to discuss some drastic geological changes that have been taking place over the last year. I know that we have already been bombarded with everything imaginable. If you look in your folders you'll see some satellite photos. Side by side comparison of this year and last," he explained. "A few things of importance I want to note. The mountain range on the California and Nevada border has raised over ninety-seven feet in elevation and expanded thirty feet at the base. This happens when plates collide, that's how our mountains are formed. Typically, something like this would take millions of years to happen, at most following a geological event of this magnitude, tens of thousands of years."

"We're expecting this," Aldar stated. "That's why we're doing the Noah. Are you saying the timeline may be moving up?"

Nate nodded. "In some areas, yes. It may change, I'm hoping it will. If not, we will have to relocate tens of millions more. Captain Henning, you joked that Houston is the earthquake capital of the world."

"I did," Curt said. "Because it is. We've had more seismic activity than anywhere else on Earth since all this began."

"You know what the reason is, right?" Nate asked.

Curt shrugged. "I am guessing newly developed fault lines."

"These are tectonic quakes. Look at image four."

Aldar and Curt both shuffled to the image of the state.

"Prior to everything," Nate said, "North America shifted two inches a year. Australia four inches a year. It's slow enough to not be noticed and not make a difference in our lifetime. Or was. Now North America shifts about a foot a year; it is increasing by twelve percent each year. This is why we have the earthquakes everywhere. It's predictable. However, even though the continent has moved a foot last year, the coast of Texas has extended into the gulf. We lost our islands two years ago, and in another ten years, Houston itself will be uninhabitable. It will be part of the gulf.

"How is that possible?" someone asked. "This isn't the intel we have been following. I realize everything changes and can change. Excuse my ignorance, this isn't my forte, but is the gulf rising faster than the ocean?"

Nate shook his head. "No, parts of Texas and Louisiana are moving faster than the rest of the continent. The disappearance of much of the Rio Grande in Brownsville confirms it."

Aldar slowly glanced up from the image. "It's breaking off."

"That's correct, Colonel," said Nate. "By my calculations, about eighty-three thousand square miles will detach. And unlike a lot of other events, *that* is something we *will* see in our lifetime."

THREE

It wasn't always called Paradise West, Virginia. It had only recently acquired the name since it was one of very few places untouched by the recent surge of nature's fury.

Rey was given very little time to prepare and she still wasn't sure what she was preparing for. The essay contest awarded her some sort of major prize which required her to immediately leave her job. Instructions were for her to pack as she would be gone for a while. No other explanation was given. The next morning, before the sun had even risen, a car showed up to take her on the three-hour drive.

Had it not been a NASA official and a military man showing up, Rey probably wouldn't have gone. She knew it had to be big and important.

Then again, what else did she have going on?

She traveled a highway, then into a mountainous area with winding roads and continuous ear popping from the increase in altitude.

When she arrived at Paradise it was heavily guarded with signs indicating it was a government installation. In fact, it was more of a base. Rey was privileged to see only one part of it; the rest was off limits for the time being.

She was in the section with several nondescript buildings, one of which was a housing unit. She was given a large private room with her own bath. The room was divided by furnishings. A bed in the corner by the window, a desk opposite of that and by the door was a couch, chair and coffee table. A small bookshelf was next to the bathroom. Basic, minimalistic, and clean. She barely had time once she arrived to unpack her bags. She was whisked off to another building where she underwent eight hours of medical testing. It was rigorous, every bit of her body, physically and emotionally, was scrutinized.

There was a small cafeteria on the first floor of her housing building that served three meals at certain times. She also had access to a kitchenette that was fully stocked.

It was almost as if the powers that be had laid out a plan to keep her occupied. The next few days consisted of physical training, along with two classes. She was the only student in both. The first class was with a teacher named Benedict Vonn, or Ben for short, and it was a class on the basics of electronics. In the other class, her teacher was a captain in the army, Sandra, who instructed her on applicable field medicine. Both were on opposite sides of the spectrum, and neither instructor told her why she was being given the classes, only that they were ongoing.

After five days, she was physically exhausted from fourteen-hour days, and mentally pushed to the limit on being kept in the dark.

She did have an idea on why she was there, she just didn't know what part she would play. Since her essay was on saving the world, she knew it had to do with that.

No one on the planet was kept in the dark.

Before it all began, it was no secret that the earth was in the middle of the Holocene Extinction. The sixth extinction event. It had begun eleven thousand years earlier and was predicted to end tens of thousands of years in the future, with at least eighty percent of all species rendered extinct.

The human species wouldn't make it that long.

Natural disasters increased with intensity. Each hurricane season was worse than the previous. Then it was proven that the earth's core had heated, causing oceanic volcanic eruptions. The oceans heated and rose. The floor of the oceans shifted, as well as the tectonic plates of the globe. A major continental drift was underway. Typically, it would take a million years to complete, however it was accelerated. In ten thousand years the face of the globe would change.

That was the future.

The now was more pressing.

The heated oceans caused major storm disturbances and unbearable heat. There were places below the equator that were dangerous for human survival. Within a few years of the change, eastern seaboard cities in the United States began to flood, the southernmost tip of Florida was submerged, and the water never receded.

Mass evacuations were made in order to preserve life. Tent cities were commonplace, and the farming industry took a nosedive. Agriculture production dropped thirty percent and diseases rose. The already over-populated Earth was slowly starving and suffocating from the changing climate.

It was predicted that unless another major event shifted the world back on track, the planet would be unhabitual for human life in three hundred years.

No one really said what that major event was. Rey

always figured it was something that would cull the population.

Still, despite the warnings, there wasn't any urgency. After all, who would be alive to care what happened three hundred years in the future?

Her presence at the so-called Noah Project told her that possibly something was being done.

She thought about it all, a lot. It's all she could do. She had no phone, no internet, and only classic books. Though she physically welcomed the time off she was given, on the sixth day she was bored.

It was during that boredom when Ben Vonn knocked on her door and told her she was needed in a meeting. He took her to office building A, then left. After a few moments, Tom Waite, the man from NASA that she met at the school, arrived.

"My apologies Miss Harper for leaving you in the dark for so long," Tom said. "I wanted to be the one to explain it all to you. Unfortunately, I was held up with the test flights of Omni-4. Are you familiar?"

"With the Omni. Yes," she said. "It's the space craft of the Corp."

"Brilliant crafts. You know the design has been around for decades, even before the shuttle. Something that generation only saw in science fiction movies. Every time I see one land or take off, I think of our heroic shuttle astronauts and how they would be in awe of our program today. It hasn't really been that long."

"No, it hasn't."

"Okay, so ... the reason you are here. You are well

aware of the dire circumstances of the earth. The first order of business is to save humanity. To save the species. The best way to do this is to find a new home. We needed ideas, hence the essays." He handed her a photo. "This is a prototype."

Rey looked down at the picture of a large ship. It looked more like a cruise ship, only gray. Rectangular in shape, narrowing in at the bottom like a boat.

"That is one of eight being constructed in the United States. Other countries are constructing similar ones," he explained. "On the positive side, these will house nearly six percent of the United States population. You and I, however, won't be around to see the completion. More than likely, those who aren't even born yet will be the passengers. They are decades away from completion and the propulsion system could take as much as forty years. The plan is to have them in space fifty years from now."

"Fifty years. I see why you said you and I won't be around."

"Even if we were, I doubt we'd get a seat. It would be a waste to take anyone older than sixty or even fifty. And those chosen would be those who could highly contribute. The plan is to evacuate and relocate those who remain. All in hopes that those who stay behind will somehow beat the odds."

"Life finds a way," Rey said.

Tom smiled slightly and nodded. "A famous quote. And you used it in your essay. Remember."

"I do."

"You also mentioned the ARCs, such as the ones we are building, along with the selection process. To paraphrase your essay, you spoke about the ARCs being in space until the Androski Wormhole opened up. It opens up every twenty or thirty years, stays open for a couple months and closes. You theorized that it would take the ARCs to another part of space where they could find a new Earth. You were much more specific, but basically that's what you wrote."

"Androski believed that the wormhole he discovered was large enough for a space craft," Rey said. "Typically, wormholes are tiny and would crush whatever tried to pass through them."

"The reason you won was because not only were you right about the ARCS, and the wormhole, you were right about your theory about there being another habitable planet just on the other side."

Rey sat up with interest. "Is there?"

Tom pushed a tablet her way and swiped his way through to the pictures. The images were that of a planet. Very little cloud cover. From the images it appeared to have one large land mass and several smaller ones around it. "These are satellite pictures taken of the actual planet. Sixty-two percent of the planet is comprised of water. The land mass is about twenty percent desert, and the rest looks pretty fertile, almost untouched. While we are not seeing signs of life, we are seeing the possibilities of a previous civilization."

"Where is it?" Rey asked.

"We don't know."

"How is that possible, you have satellite photos, which means you can tell where …"

Tom shook his head. "In 1993, the National Ocean and

29

Atmospheric Administration launched the number thirteen satellite. They lost contact with NOAA Thirteen a couple of days later and assumed it was destroyed. Four weeks ago, it returned out of nowhere, and transmitted these photos. That's when we confirmed it was by the Androski Wormhole. We believe the satellite went through the wormhole and was unable to return pictures to us until it was pulled back out again."

"So all those deep space probes and it was a weather satellite that discovered another planet. N-O-A-A. Noah."

"Yes, and if you think about it, the name fits everything. The ARCs, the starting over ... the planet. But because of the weather satellite, our information about this planet is limited."

"I would think." Rey looked at the pictures again. "This is amazing."

"What's amazing is, with Androski, we have the ability to go there. To see if it is a viable option. We have located Androski."

Slowly, Rey lifted her eyes to him. "You know where it is?"

"And it is in the same place Androski theorized. Everything he theorized is true. The slow closing. According to our calculations, the daily decrease will leave the wormhole impassible in about three months. So ... we are sending a crew there in two weeks aboard Omni-4."

"You don't know how far inside the wormhole the planet is located."

Tom shook his head. "No, we don't. We can only hope that it's close. Close enough to allow a scouting crew to land."

"And I get to be witness to all of this," Rey said. "Thank you."

"You'll be more than that," Tom told her. "You'll be part of the crew. Congratulations. You're going to Noah."

FOUR

"Paradise, this is Omni-4, making atmosphere approach," Curt made the radio call, reaching above him for the controls.

"Copy that, Omni-4, you are clear, make your approach. Over."

"Making approach, final landing before Noah," said Curt.

"Heat shields up," Aldar stated.

"Heat shields up," Curt repeated. "Switching to full auto. Music on ..."

"No." Aldar reached up and stopped him. "Please. No. If I have to listen to 'Fox on the Run' one more time."

"It's a great landing and takeoff song," Curt defended.

"So why play it when flying?" Aldar asked.

Curt shrugged. "It's a great song."

"I like the original better."

"Ha!"

"Gentlemen." Ben Vonn turned his chair slightly. "Please don't tell me the Noah is going to be like this the whole time."

"There will be a balance." Curt looked at him. "Those

remaining three chairs will be filled. Speaking of which ... what's she like?"

Aldar groaned.

"What?" Curt asked. "Why the reaction?"

"Just seemed to me to have subtle 'should I hit on her?' tones," Aldar commented.

"That's hysterical." Curt laughed. "Seriously. No. We're going to be spending two weeks with her, I'm wondering."

"Quiet," replied Ben. "Very quiet. I don't know if that's her personality, or she just didn't have anything to say. I don't know much about her. She didn't volunteer that info."

"We'll find out soon enough." Aldar indicated with a nod of his head that they were making their approach.

He made sure they were locked in, heat shields working, and they headed into Earth's atmosphere.

"Decades ago, NASA began the design of the IXS Enterprise," Tom explained to Rey as they walked through the hanger. "They actually started building it."

"Enterprise. Like *Star Trek*?"

"Yes. It bore a resemblance. It was the hope that by now, we'd have warp drive."

"Unless I'm wrong, something like that isn't needed for this mission."

"You're correct," Tom said. "For this we need sustainability if a suitable second planet is not found. The IXS was bulky, relying on the 'spin' factor to simulate the gravity you see in sci-fi movies. The Omni, however, is quite different. It's a smaller deal, made for short exploratory missions. It's not bulky, its propulsion system is fusion, and drive is ionic so it doesn't need those large tanks. You still have to go through that phase of training for weightlessness and the pressure of takeoff."

"I'm ready."

"I'm sure you are." Tom led them to the airfield. "And if you are also ready … you're about to meet the pilots of the mission. Colonel Finch and Captain Henning."

"The Clutch."

Tom smiled. "The Clutch." He gave Rey a pat to the back as they stood staring at the horizon, waiting on Omni-4 to land.

She had not seen a picture of either of them, nor had Rey heard much about Finch and Henning, other than seeing The Clutch in the news.

But she knew instantly by their demeanor which man was which. And that came before they spoke a word.

As the three men walked her way, she immediately eliminated Ben Vonn. She knew him from class.

The other two men were both taller than Vonn, the same height, and about a decade apart in age.

One man walked confident, almost cocky, with a smile on his face, the other reserved and strong.

With hair clipped so close to his head he appeared almost bald in the sun, the tall man extended his hand and said, "Pleasure to meet you, ma'am."

Finch.

Rey guessed he was Colonel Finch and she was correct. There was a strength about him. In his handshake, his eyes, and the sound of his voice.

The other man flashed a boyish grin when he removed his cap. His light brown hair was a mess and with a simple, "Hey there," as his greeting, Rey knew he could be none other than a man they called The Clutch.

"And you know Major Vonn." Tom pointed to Ben. "He's been guiding you on electronics. The other two members of the crew are Captain Sandra Anderson, our Medical Specialist, whom you met, and Dr. Gale, who is out in the field and should be here tomorrow."

"Bet you're excited," The Clutch said.

"Nervous. Scared," Rey replied.

"Well whatever you need to know," Finch said, "we'll be happy to help. I read your essay. It was amazing, ma'am."

"Rey. Call me Rey," she said.

"Like the sun?" Clutch joked.

"Really?" Finch looked at him.

Tom cleared his throat. "Now that the introductions are over, Miss Harper will be joining us in the debriefing before her training gets tough today. I expect you gentlemen to assist her as best as possible," he said. "And of course, for the love of God ... behave."

FIVE

Rey tried to determine if not eating was detrimental. At least if she had eaten, she would have had something to throw up after weightlessness training.

They told her it was a bit more extreme than usual, but she'd appreciate the torturous drill after it was all said and done. She didn't see how that was possible, she could barely walk. Everything spun and even the medicated patch they gave her didn't help.

Colonel Finch told her that it would take a couple of hours to recover. Rey thought she'd lay down before the meeting, but that made things worse. Her bed moved worse than after any night of drinking. She was just glad the debriefing had been before the training. It was rather boring to her, with the exception of the talk about the wormhole. Somehow, in her mind, she never imagined a wormhole could be seen. It wasn't like it was some black hole. But The Clutch called the sight of it, "Dangerous."

"You can't see it," Clutch explained. *"Not from a distance, and you can only see it from a certain angle."*

"So there's a chance of missing it?" Tom asked.

Clutch shook his head. "No, we know where it is. We won't miss it."

"So why is it dangerous?"

"Because we have no idea what's behind it," he replied. "I'm not talking after we go through. I'm talking about now. What's behind it? What could be behind it? Right now, it's like a wall in space. When that thing disappears, what will appear?"

"Fortunately," Finch explained, "space is infinite and vast. That wormhole is miniscule in the scope of things, so the probability of an object making an Earth approach, right there, behind it is extremely low. But Captain Henning brings up a valid point and one that future generations should consider when it returns."

Rey wasn't a rocket scientist or an astronaut, so she asked, "It's a wormhole. Did you guys not go behind it? I would think, yes, it's a wall, but I would think a thin one."

"You would think, Ms. Harper," Finch replied. "But we tried. It's like a dead spot that has created a density in space which we couldn't get by. Think of it like a funnel, yes you can go through the opening, but you can't get into the funnel by the sides. It's complicated; when you see it up close, you'll understand. Pictures don't do it justice."

That conversation at the debriefing stayed on her mind. The pictures taken by the Omni showed an area with a slight rippling, that was it. The thought of it was frightening, and the more she thought about it, the more questions she had.

"There is a reason all of you have been chosen." Tom paced around the oval table in the meeting room. "I'm talking beyond the qualifications you have."

Aldar Finch watched him pace then looked about the faces around the table. Curt kept fidgeting in his chair, swiveling it left to right. Reyanne took notes, or rather, was ready to. Ben Vonn was like Finch. A company man, no nonsense, and the best damn engineer he knew. If anything mechanical were to go wrong, he wanted no one else but Vonn on board.

He was about as familiar with the woman Sandra as he was with Rey. A no-makeup kind of woman, with a physically strong build, wearing her dark brown hair tightly pulled back. She was an army physician, and as far as space experience … she had only been in the simulator. Aldar understood the reasoning for her presence on the mission. They were about to possibly step foot on another planet, a foreign terrain, medically they needed to have everything covered.

That left Nathan Gale; Aldar knew him well. Nathan had been instrumental in the mission before it was even finalized, before even Aldar himself knew about it. He was a brilliant geologist and physicist, who had also done extensive work in archeology. He had a folder before him, and no doubt there was something in there vital that he was going to share. His fingers fiddled with the edges of the folder anxiously as if he was just waiting for the moment to flip it open.

"Each of you were also chosen because …" Tom continued. "Your lack of emotional responsibility here at home."

A strange thing happened in the after second of Tom's statement. Four people at that table, Sandra, Rey, Ben, and Nathan all slightly lowered their heads, looking down in thought, maybe even loss. All of their faces screamed as if they were all saying, *Yeah, well, no emotional responsibility? We didn't really have a choice.*

"For several of you," Tom said, "I am sorry about that. It is vital though that emotional attachments and responsibilities be at an absolute minimum."

Curt mumbled slightly audibly. "Yep. If no one cares about us, there'll be no one to miss us if we don't come back."

It was a hard truth that Aldar knew well.

Tom cleared his throat. "That's rather harsh, but we're confident that isn't the case."

"Not to make anyone doubtful," Curt said. "I'm going no matter what. However, what about Naamah?"

"Naamah?" Sandra asked. "Biblically that's what they say Noah's wife's name was."

Tom nodded. "Because the project is called The Noah, we named a satellite Naamah. We sent it into the wormhole six weeks ago and lost contact. Which ... would theoretically be normal considering we don't know to what part of the universe that wormhole will take us. It hasn't returned as programmed. And just like we are not in communication with the satellite, we will not be in communication with you after you pass through. Once you go through, you are on your own. But in the capable hands of Colonel Finch and Captain Henning. They'll get you there, land, and get you back."

Aldar spoke up. "I am confident in the abilities of the Omni to handle it. It's just the landing, and where we will land. Yes, the NOAA-13 took the photos, but we don't know how far into the wormhole it traveled until it arrived. We could run right into the planet or not see it at all."

"What if it's not there?" Rey asked. "Then what?"

Ben answered, "Meaning no disrespect to the colonel, but it has to be close enough to the wormhole that it is visible. Enough that the NOAA was pulled to it. If it's not visible, we will need to turn around and come back. There'll be no way to gauge where the wormhole is again if we venture too far away."

"It's there. It's close, I feel it," Nathan said. "The only problem I see, is what side of the planet we see on arrival. Is it day? Is it night? And as far as landing, I have a good idea on where we can land. I have been working extensively with these satellite photos."

"And he has more photos than we've shown," Tom said. "What we are about to discuss, what is in those photos is highly classified. Even upon your return there is information you cannot divulge. Nathan?"

Nathan opened the folder. "We believe at one time the planet not only had inhabitants, but a highly advanced civilization. There are no clear-cut cities or ruins on the photos …" He began to pass them around. "But I have circled what I believe are structures emerging from the ground. Buried. They have to have been big. It's hard to say how long ago this civilization went extinct, but whatever happened, happened fast. I mean … days. Buried as fast, and perhaps deeper, than Pompeii."

"If we let it out that an intelligent life existed on another planet," Tom said, "it could hit the morals of a lot of the population."

"Doubt in God," Rey added. "People believed God created life here on Earth. If there's life elsewhere, that faith could be shattered."

"Lack of faith …" Tom lifted his shoulders. "Lack of re-percussions for actions. With a world slowly dying, fear of God and what will happen in the afterlife controls a lot of people. No fear of a hell, who is to say what could become of law and order while we're trying to save mankind."

"Any guesses as to what happened?" Aldar asked

Nathan.

"Not really. We have to get down there and see. Natural disasters, comet, meteor … war. We'll know when we land, if, of course, the atmosphere is conducive to us being there. Our suits will only afford us so much time on the surface. If the surface isn't toxic. We'll know when we get there. It's a guessing game."

"It's our hope that the team can land and be on the surface for two weeks. Learning not only as much as you can about the planet, but possibly try to find out what happened to the inhabitants there as well. Perhaps finding out how and why they all died can be a clue to help us save as many as we can here."

"Then what?" Sandra asked. "Say we get there. The place is great. Then what?"

"We prepare for the next time the Androski opens back up. When it does we send colonists to start preparing the planet for the arrival of the ARCs. Which should be ready by the next opening."

It was all science fiction to Aldar. Then again, when he was a boy, he wouldn't have imagined a space craft such as the Omni. In fifty years anything was possible.

He stared down at the picture handed to him. A red circle outlined something in the trees. He stared and examined it and didn't see what Nathan was talking about. The object could have been anything. To Aldar, the planet looked virgin, untouched, beautiful and lush. Actually, to Aldar, it looked too good to be true.

A little tavern twenty miles from the base served an amazing steak and rib special. Tom had taken the crew to dinner in the hopes of building a comradery. But the evening of dinner followed by drinks was cut short and the mood nosedived when the news of yet another earthquake in Houston came on the television. It was by far the most devastating, leaving most of the city in ruins, and the projected death toll in the tens of thousands.

Rey's mood was the only one unchanged. She had been quiet and even-keeled since the meeting. The news of the quake, although sad, was not a shock. Gone were the days when the news was filled with stories of murder, crime, and political rhetoric. It was replaced with continuous stories of disaster and death. It was one quake after another. Storm after storm. Volcanoes erupting for months on end. The world was literally falling apart in order for nature to start anew.

The ride back to the base was a somber one.

Once in her room, Rey opened the bottle of whiskey that Tom had given to her. She poured about two inches into a glass and walked to the window to stare out at the clear sky.

She'd be up there soon. It was so vast. Someone once said to her that if she thought too much about the infinity of space she would go insane. That sounded true because as she looked at the star-speckled sky, it was mind blowing to even consider there was no end. It went on forever.

Rey missed her phone. She missed the internet. If she had them, she'd be researching and looking up everything.

A knock at her door drew her from her thoughts, and she walked over to answer it.

Aldar Finch stood at her door.

"Ms. Harper, I am sorry to knock so late."

"It's not late. Come in." She opened the door wider.

"Thank you, ma'am."

"Stop," she said. "Rey. Call me Rey, Colonel."

"Rey." He nodded. "Please. Call me Al or Finch."

"I will, thank you. Drink?" she asked and pointed to the bottle.

"Um ... yes, please, thank you."

Rey walked over to her desk and poured him a glass. "Tom got me this bottle."

"Tom got us all one. Thank you." He accepted the drink.

"What brings you here?"

"I don't mean to be intrusive. I don't. I just wanted to make sure you were alright."

"I'll be okay. There's a ton on my mind."

"I know this is a lot to take in. I have had decades of training and it makes me nervous."

"Nervous is an understatement for me."

"I understand. There's been no time for adjustment for you. We're all ... the rest of the team has a different mindset. You ... you are, and please don't take this the wrong way, you're a public relations insertion."

"Wow. I ... didn't think of it like that."

"Please. I'm not being disrespectful, I'm merely inferring to the fact that this was just thrown at you. And I am being long-winded here. My point ... I'm here. If you need to talk, if you need anything, let me know. We are on this team

43

together."

"Thank you. That means ..." She paused when she noticed his eyes shifted to the photos on her desk. "Colonel?"

"I'm ... I'm sorry. I was ..." He lifted the picture of Rey and a group of people. "Your family?"

Rey nodded. "And this ..." She lifted the other picture of her and her husband. "My husband."

"I just thought we all ..."

"No emotional attachments?" she asked. "Yeah. Everyone in this photo"—she pointed to the group—"they're gone. My husband as well. The flood that wiped out Canonsburg ten months ago took my family."

"I ... I am so sorry."

"Me, too." Rey took a deep breath then slowly released it. "I have a brother. When I said I had a lot on my mind. He's it. Right on top. I ... I didn't even get to say goodbye to him. I mean I did in a sense. I told him I won an essay contest with NASA and was going to collect my prize." She faked a soft chuckle. "I didn't even know what being part of 'The Noah' meant. I didn't know I would be going into space, through a wormhole with a chance I would never get back, never come home. They brought me here, took my phone, cut me off. Now ... I'm leaving, and I can't even say goodbye properly, tell him, or my nephew and niece one last time that I love them. I can't ..." She paused when she saw Aldar reach into his pocket and pull out his phone.

He held it up. "They didn't take mine." He extended it to her.

Rey's eyes lit up. "Thank you. Thank you so much." The second she reached for it, he stopped her.

"Listen. I know it's a lot of unknowns. But we will make it back here."

"Do you … do you really believe that?" she asked.

"I do," he said with certainty. "I believe that. One hundred percent. We will make it home." Aldar released his hand and allowed for her to take the phone. With his drink in hand, he stepped from her room to give her privacy.

PART TWO: THE STORIES

SIX

He never intended to be an air force career man, the reserves worked well for him. But when Ben couldn't secure a good paying job right after his son was born, he figured, 'what the heck' and went to full-time active duty.

It paid off.

He never really had to move his family much and he liked his job working on planes. However, his mechanical talents kept him climbing the difficulty roster and he went from planes to NASA where he eventually helped build the Omni. He knew the Omni backwards and forwards. Could figure out any problem that arose, though there weren't many.

He understood the 'why' of things, therefore he could figure out the 'how' when needed.

That wasn't the only reason he was brought on for The Noah Project.

Other than working for NASA, Ben lived a pretty normal life. He had a house right outside the base in a gated community. A four-bedroom home with four bathrooms. His wife, Anna boasted about the bathrooms, claiming that her and Ben having their own was what kept their marriage sane.

She was a very basic, easy-to-please woman. Ben met her when he was eighteen and they married when he was twenty. They had two sons, Ben who was seventeen, and Josh who was fifteen. He was a hands-on father and vowed he wouldn't let his boys fall into the lazy and useless phase. Ben started teaching his boys to do things early in life. That wasn't to say they liked it.

He supposed they'd rather be playing video games or be with their friends.

When Ben wasn't working he was with his family and he wanted them with him.

"Benny, you paying attention?" Ben asked his son. They were in the driveway that afternoon with the front of the car jacked off, the wheel removed.

"Yeah, how can I not. It's boring."

"Be that as it may, it's useful."

"Dad, really," Benny said. "Why do I need to know how to change brake pads?"

"Because one day in the future, your wife is going to say to you the brakes are making a noise."

"So I'll take it to a shop."

"That's the problem these days," Ben said. "No one knows how to work on their own cars."

"That's because they're all computers now. Not like when pap was young."

"Brakes are brakes, tires are tires, some things don't change. Now come on down here and put this pad on."

"It's Liz's graduation party, I need to go."

"Well, I have to drive you, right?" Ben asked. "Can't take

you without the brakes on."

"What about Mom's car?"

"What about helping me?"

The younger Ben groaned and joined his father on the ground.

In fact, he groaned when they were finished too, stomping in the house, through the kitchen.

"Now, I'm dirty," he complained. "Can one of you take me after I clean up? Please. Thank you." He walked from the kitchen.

Anna paused in cleaning the stove top. "I'll take him."

"You sure?" Ben asked, gabbing a juice. "I just want to take a quick shower and then we can go. He can wait."

"You forget what it's like to be a teenage boy," Anna said. "No, no, I'll take him. I want to …"

A slight rumble of the ground caused the dishes to rattle and Anna to stop. She held on. "Was that an earthquake?" she asked.

"Probably. They're commonplace." He set down the glass.

The younger Ben flew into the kitchen. "Was that an earthquake?"

"Yes," Ben replied. "Like I told your mother, they're commonplace."

"Here in Kentucky?" Benny questioned. "Never felt one before."

"There's always a first time."

"Cool." Again, Benny ran from the kitchen, this time calling out, "Hey, Josh! Dad said it was a quake."

51

Ben shook his head with a laugh. "I'm hitting the shower. You'll probably be gone by the time I get out." He leaned in and kissed her.

"I need to stop at the store."

Ben lifted his hand as he walked away, his sign that he acknowledged what she said. He could hear the boys talking excitedly about the quake as he made his way up the stairs. He walked in the bedroom, then straight to the bathroom and started the shower. The water always needed to run a little bit to get to optimum temperature. While that ran, he picked out his change of clothes, laying them on the bed.

The steam from the shower flowed out of the open bathroom door and Ben kicked off his shoes and lifted his shirt over his head. Just as he tossed that on the floor, a loud squeal then clanking pipe sound rang out and he noticed the water just stopped.

"What the hell?"

He walked to the bathroom and as soon as he crossed the arch of the door, the entire floor jolted violently once, sending Ben slamming hard into the doorjamb.

He lost his balance for a second, but as soon as he stood, the floor jolted again. It moved hard with a creaking sound. Within a second, a loud cracking sound rang out, and Ben shook as the floor slanted fifteen degrees, sending him off his footing to the carpet and rolling into the bed.

"Anna!" he yelled. "Ben! Josh! Get out of the house!"

He stumbled to his feet as the house shook and jolted.

"Everyone!" He flew from the bedroom. "Get out of the house!"

It was a two story, with an open upstairs hallway before

the staircase.

When he emerged into the hall, the boys were coming out of the bedroom.

"Dad?" Josh, his youngest held on to the upper railing. "Dad? What's going on?"

"Josh, give me your hand." Ben held out this hand. "Hold on to your bother and my hand."

"Ben!" Anna cried out.

Ben turned his head as Anna struggled to make it up the staircase. What the hell was she thinking? "Anna!" he yelled. "Get out of the house. Now!"

"We … we can't!" she cried. "We can't. The street is gone. There's nothing out …"

"What do you mean …" Another crack and another jolt, the house leaned even more and Anna lost her footing.

He turned from reaching for his son, lunged down a couple of steps, and grabbed hold of Anna's arm, securing her. "Boys, now." With his free hand he reached outward for his sons to come to him.

That was when it happened. One loud rumble, the house shook violently, and with a bang and smashing sound the house leaned as if tilting on its side.

Not only was Ben losing his stance, Anna was falling as the house tilted downward.

Ben gripped the railing and tightened his hold on Anna a split second before the entire house turned ninety degrees. It slammed hard, and as if it were made of matchsticks. The front of the house broke off, falling into what seemed like an endless pit.

He couldn't even see where the rest of the house went.

A hollowness, long, deep, and dark.

A second later, with a horrifying scream, he watched his oldest son sail downward.

"No!" Ben screamed out. "No!"

Benny fell out of sight. His arms failing as he tried to swim in the air, unsuccessfully trying to stop.

One more jolt and his younger son followed.

Ben couldn't scream enough. It was a nightmare, it couldn't be real. A dream he had to wake from.

He was head first toward that pit as well, one hand holding onto the railing while his leg twisted around a post, keeping him there.

He had Anna by the wrist, but she didn't hold onto him. Below her was nothing, nothing but a long fall to death. She dangled, feet kicking while she cried in agony.

He didn't have that strong of a hold.

"Anna, stop moving!" he shouted.

"Let me go!" she screamed. "My boys, my boys, let me go! Oh, God, Ben, let me go!"

He didn't know how long he could hold onto her. One more jolt was all it would take and they'd both fall to their deaths, just as their sons had. Even though she begged him to release her, Ben couldn't let go. He'd hold on as long as he could. At that moment, she was all he had left.

Ben sat in the twelfth-floor lounge of the hospital. His arm was in a sling; he had pulled out his shoulder and torn ligaments in his arm. It hurt, but the pain was nothing compared to what he felt in his soul.

He couldn't process what had just happened. The reality of it was still lost. He kept grabbing the phone to call the boys and tell them he was waiting on them to admit Anna.

But, there were no sons to call.

They were gone.

How long did he hold on to Anna?

It probably wasn't as long as it seemed. He was ready to give up. Ready to let go and allow him and Anna to join the boys when a neighbor yelled out, "Hold on, we're gonna help."

It was Jason, their next-door neighbor; he served in the air force with Ben. One second Ben was holding his wife, the next he saw Jason with a rope cautiously making his way across the railing of the second floor toward Ben.

How did he get there? How did he get on the second floor of his house?

He tied the rope on Ben's leg.

"He's secure!" Jason called out. "Ben. Hey, Ben, we have you. Just hold on to Anna. Hold her. You're good. Let go of the railing and secure her. We'll pull you both up."

Ben felt the rope on his foot. He didn't fear falling if he let go, because he didn't care, and he knew Anna didn't either.

He let go of the railing, quickly grabbing onto Anna's other wrist. He slipped a little, but he felt the resistance of the rope.

There had to be more people than Jason. Ben couldn't see. They pulled him up, and never once did he loosen his grip on Anna. His hands were like super glue.

The railing didn't hold during the rescue. Halfway across it gave away. It broke off, once again sending Anna dangling.

She didn't scream or squirm. At some point she passed out and was dead weight.

When they finally pulled them to safety, there was a group of people who were involved in the rescue effort. Ben was in shock. He held on to Anna, keeping her in his arms. He wanted to thank them but couldn't even muster the words. When he was on solid ground, he was able to look back.

Jason's house was intact, unfazed. The destruction began at Ben's. One part of his home was gone. The section of the second floor was all that remained, caught on the edge of the huge gaping hole that consumed everything in their housing plan after his house.

It wasn't until he was at the hospital he learned what had actually happened, and that was from the news.

It wasn't an earthquake.

It was a sinkhole.

They were calling it the biggest one in United States history. Something snapped and the ground just gave out.

The sinkhole consumed sixteen homes. Those who were in their homes were swallowed, only Ben and Anna survived.

"Major Vonn," a voice called to him.

Ben looked up to the woman in scrubs that stood before him.

"We have your wife situated in 1218. You can go see

her now. We just gave her a sedative for the evening."

"Thank you." Ben stood and slowly walked from the lounge down the hall. Quietly he stepped into his wife's room. Anna lay on the bed, her forearm draped across her head as she stared at the window.

"Anna ..."

"Go away."

"Anna, please ..."

"Why?" she sobbed the word. "Why didn't you let me die?"

"I couldn't. I ... I couldn't do that. You're my wife. I love you."

"If you loved me, you would have let me go."

"Anna ..."

"Please, leave. I want to sleep."

"I'll be back," Ben whispered. He knew she had been given a sedative, it probably was kicking in. "I'm going to go to the vending machine."

Anna merely nodded.

Hands in his pocket, feeling the weight of his loss, Ben walked from the room.

He had made it all the way down to the vending area on the first floor, and studied the contents of the machine, when he realized he didn't have any money. He didn't have his wallet or phone. It was the final straw, the breaking point ... Ben cracked, angrily he drew his fist back, ready to slam it into the machine in a fit of overwhelming sadness when he heard the eruptions of screams.

What now? Ben thought. *What could it be now?*

Medical workers flew by him, people were still screaming. Ben walked toward the commotion to see what was happening.

Everyone was running outside.

As he crossed through the automatic glass doors, he heard a man shouting. "Everyone back up. Stay back."

A large group of people encircled something. Ben walked toward them and stopped when he saw the bare legs on the ground.

"What happened?" a woman asked. "Did she fall?"

Figuring he'd seen enough death for the day, he turned away.

"No, she jumped. I saw her jump."

Ben froze.

He lifted his head to scan the building.

No, he thought. *No*.

He spun back around quickly and barged toward the crowd. He pushed his way against the grain and when he finally broke through he saw the victim. Twisted legs behind her back, her neck contorted, eyes open, and head encircled in a pool of blood.

Clearly, she had jumped.

But it wasn't a stranger, it wasn't some random woman … it was Anna.

SEVEN

They were twins, but as they got older people started calling them the hero twins because of what they did for careers. Their careers weren't the only thing similar in their lives, everything Sandra and Sarah Anderson did was similar. It was more on purpose than coincidence, they preferred it that way.

They were born three weeks early, not much when it came to a multiple birth, and surprisingly they weren't just healthy, they were a solid birth weight. No one could believe they were early.

Identical twins born six minutes apart, the girls could never be more than a few hours apart their entire childhood.

When policy in school dictated they were to be in separate classes, the girls were physically ill, so their father took a second job to send them to a small Catholic school.

They were the only children to older parents, who had tried for a long time to have children. Both were tomboyish and athletic. They played softball all through their teenage years. Sandra the pitcher, Sarah the catcher.

They both went to the same college, then both enlisted in the army. It was there, after basic training they spent their

59

longest time apart. Sandra finished her medical degree, while Sarah worked search and rescue. Yet, after their training they worked and deployed together.

But their parents weren't getting any younger, and instead of re-enlisting full time, Sandra and Sarah joined the civilian workforce and served in the reserves. Sarah took an instructor position at Wildland Fire Academy, while Sandra worked in the emergency room. Both were north of their home in Los Angeles.

No more deployments. No more worries of dangers for their parents.

So they thought.

Sandra knew that afternoon when she heard about the wildfires something was wrong or was going to happen. She had this all-consuming gut feeling of doom. She kept texting Sarah, calling her.

"I'm fine," Sarah said. "I'm not even near there."

"But they are close to Mom and Dad's," Sandra said.

"I've seen worse. You know it's bad if I have to go out there. It won't get to that, I'm almost positive."

Sarah seemed so certain, and the news didn't really depict the fire as out of control.

Sandra was on the overnight shift and it was particularly quiet. The nurses were putting up early Christmas decorations when Sandra got a message from her parents' neighbor. It prompted her to call Sarah.

"Hey, sis, it's me," she said into the voicemail. "I know you're sleeping. Just got a call from the Jamisons. They said the fire is close, they're evacuating, but Dad's on the roof with a hose. I can't leave. Let me know if you get this. I'll keep trying them."

Sandra did, she tried Sarah and her parents every twenty minutes, with no luck. In between the calls and the patients, she watched the news as deadly winds picked up forcing the fire out of control. Soon she wasn't able to call. The emergency room filled up quickly, smoke inhalation … burns.

It went from small to the worst fire in Californian history. The entire north part of Los Angeles was being evacuated, and it included the hospital.

Between patients coming in and those they tried to move out, it was insane.

Around five in the morning, Sandra experienced a sharp pain in her chest. In fact, at first she thought it was a heart attack, then she realized it was something else.

Her connection to Sarah; it was a premonition of heartache that manifested in a physical nature. Immediately, she stopped what she was doing and attempted to contact her parents. She didn't even get a ring.

After failing to reach Sarah, she found a fireman, and asked for help locating her sister and family.

All Sandra kept thinking was Sarah left to help her parents and something went wrong. Something went terribly wrong.

She was given assurances.

"Wait it out," they said. "Everyone will be fine. Your sister is an instructor."

The news reported every available person was out there battling the blaze.

The fire raged across highways, the heat of which

caused collapses while the flames swallowed cars and the smoke choked the life out of anyone on foot.

It moved rapidly, and with the winds it was a force of destruction and heat nearly equivalent to a volcanic eruption.

Hours turned into days, days turned into weeks.

Once the fires had ceased and the cinders snuffed out, Sandra went to her parents' home.

It was gone.

Destroyed.

Sandra's apartment not far away was also destroyed.

There were no signs of their cars at either home.

Despite searching, despite looking at the remains of every unidentified person ... Sandra never heard or saw her family again.

EIGHT

"Daddy, Pappy said we're going fishing today." Gin-Gin had her mother's big blue eyes and blonde hair. Every time Nathan looked at his four-year-old daughter, he saw the face of his wife who said she was going to bingo one evening when Gin-Gin was nine months old, and never returned. Before the police could be notified, she called and said she was fine and not coming back.

Nathan got a card in the mail two months later stating she wasn't cut out for that life. He was hurt, but he moved on. After all, he had Gin-Gin, and she was all that mattered.

His Associate Director's position at the United States Geological Survey Agency took him all over the country. When he could he brought his daughter along with his mother to help. For the most part his parents were a godsend. They had Gin-Gin a lot and Nathan often stayed at their home in Meredith, New Hampshire for weeks on end, especially when he had to work out of Boston or Concord.

"It finally stopped raining," Gin-Gin said brightly over her pancake breakfast.

"Did it now?" Nathan smiled, pouring a coffee into his travel mug.

Gin-Gin giggled. "You know that, silly. Pappy said it's a fishing day."

"Now, now, don't you go spreading no tales," his father said in such a New Hampshire way. "I said no such thing. I said we're going to the fishing store. It had closed for a spell." He fiddled with a fishing lure.

"Is that why you're getting your flies ready?"

"It's a lure, call it what it is. For a geo man you sure don't know much about fishing." His father stood up.

"I know enough about lakes."

"Don't make you a fisherman. Surprises me though. The whole family fishes."

"I fish." Nathan walked to his daughter, kissed her on the head, and stole a piece of her pancake.

"You sit in a chair and prop a reel. That's not fishing, that's sitting and waiting for the fish to come to you." He refreshed his mug and peered out the window. "Rain stopped good. Sun is gonna be strong."

"So does that mean my daughter is telling the truth? Are you taking her fishing or just to your shop?"

"Both. You know how I am about my store, I keep it running, so your mother will tend to it and I'll tend to the baby."

Nathan smiled. "Please watch her on the boat."

"Oh, I'll do the same to her as I did to you," he said. "Life jacket and tie you to the chair."

Nathan laughed, then whispered to his daughter, "You're in good hands." He lifted his head when he heard a 'hmm' come from his father. "What?" Nathan asked. "She's not in good hands?"

"She is," he said, distracted. "There's a mist rising on the lake."

"Dad, of course there is. You heard that rain last night. It was horrible. I'm surprised there's not a lot of damage. Plus, it's morning."

"I know mist. I've been living here my whole life. It's different than the usual morning mist."

"Dad," Nathan chuckled his name. "It's not even seven, it's the same mist."

"Come take a look."

After another kiss, Nathan walked to the kitchen window. "What am I looking at?"

"The mist. Does it look different to you? Darker?"

"It's the sun. Maybe there's a fire somewhere."

"Hmm."

"Maybe you're just looking for an excuse not to take her fishing."

"Oh, I'll take her fishing," his father said. "Maybe just not on the boat."

"I have to go. I'll call when I get to the center." He back-stepped to Gin-Gin and gave her another kiss. "I won't be late. Have fun. I love you."

"Love you too, Daddy."

Nathan grabbed his keys and slowed down when he saw his father wasn't moving. "Dad. You okay?"

"It's thickening and looks like it's rolling inland. Better get a move on, might make for dangerous driving."

"Thanks. I'm headed out now." He laid his hand on his father's back and took another look out the window. The mist had thickened, it was odd, but nothing concerning. "Tell Mom I'll call her later." After receiving a nod from his father, Nathan left the home.

"Morning Nathan." The neighbor from next door waved as he collected his paper.

"Morning," Nathan replied, waved, and got into his car. He pulled out from the front of the house with a short, quick toot of the horn and drove down the road, heading toward the highway that would take him south.

It wasn't that bad of a drive to Boston. He wished he was stopping for the day in Concord, that was a quick route. Boston was a good ninety-minute drive, but in the morning, it was closer to two hours. At least it was all highway. Nathan usually listened to older music or the talk radio, depending on his mood.

On that day, he was in 'no radio' mood until he hit about an hour into his drive, just south of Concord when he noticed two large military trucks going north on the opposite side of the road; they moved faster than the traffic. He wouldn't have thought much of it had it not been for the large convoy of White Tractor trailers, large trucks, and a few white buses all moving together, all at the same speed, traveling north.

Through the corner of his eye he spotted the FEMA decal on the side of one of the vehicles.

Nathan knew what that meant, he had seen it many times before the disasters started. He remembered when there were only ten FEMA regions. Now there were fifteen— three dedicated to Texas alone. He guessed that number would grow eventually if the federal government could keep up.

But that movement told Nathan something big had

happened.

He didn't feel any tremors, so maybe the rain storms had caused damage. Reaching out, he switched on the radio, and sure enough the computerized voice was making an announcement. It was at the end of one, so Nathan didn't have a clue what was said. Another mile down the road, hand on the radio, ready to try another station, the emergency beep alerted.

"The following roads have been closed at this time. Please seek alternative routes. Route 104 at the intersection of Pease Road. Daniel Webster Highway at College Road. Waukewan Road. Bartlett Hill Road ..."

"Jesus Christ." Nathan swerved and hit the gas when he recognized the road names all too well. "That's Meredith."

The next exit wasn't far, and he took it, turning around and getting back on the highway to head back.

What happened in that area?

"Come on, Dad, pick up, pick up." He spoke to himself after not getting an answer. "Call Mom's house phone," he instructed the car. It dialed. No answer. "Call the bait shop."

Same thing.

No answer.

Nathan's heart beat out of control. The only thing that gave him any comfort was the fact that his daughter was with his parents and there wasn't a soul on the earth he trusted more than his father.

It was constant calling. Over and over as he drove as fast as he could and as far as he could until the FEMA blockade brought him to a halt.

Nothing was said over the radio. He hadn't received any alerts on his phone. The worst-case scenario in his mind was some sort of flash flood.

He pulled his car over, got out and walked to the blockade on foot.

"I'm sorry, sir." He was stopped by an armed soldier. "We can't let you go in."

"What's going on?" Nathan asked. "My family is in there."

"Sir, we have no information to release at this time."

"Look"—he pulled out his wallet—"I'm Dr. Nathan Gale of the USGS." He showed his identification. "You can let me in there."

"I'm sorry. I can't."

Frustrated and scared, Nathan walked a few feet away, pulled out his phone, and called the director.

"Nathan," Jim, the director, answered with a rush. "Is this you?"

"Yes."

"Oh, thank God."

"What's going on?" Nathan asked. "I didn't get an alert."

"Nate," Jim said. "We thought you were in Meredith."

"I was speaking in Boston today. I was on my way …"

"Nate, is your family in Meredith?"

"They were when I left. Have they evacuated? What is happening? FEMA is here, they won't let me through."

"Nate … Nate … it … we think it was a limnic eruption."

"What? That's not … that's not possible," Nathan said

in disbelief. "We have never had one here in the US."

"I know. I know. We think … no, we're pretty sure that's what it was."

"The lake isn't deep enough."

"The CO_2 levels are high. Northeast winds moved it quickly and it settled. FEMA is going in."

"You have to call them. Call FEMA. I have to go in. I'll suit up."

"Nathan, that's not a good—"

"My family is in there!" Nathan shouted, then calmed down. "I'm sorry. I'm sorry."

"No, it's alright. I understand. I'll make the call."

"Thank you." Hands shaking, Nathan placed the phone in his pocket.

There had to be a mistake. Limnic eruptions happened in deep lakes when the CO_2 in the water suddenly explodes creating a noxious cloud that suffocates and often burns the skin. Anything and anyone affected suffers a horrible, agonizing death.

He prayed that wasn't the case. If it was, then his father was right. There was something different about the mist and Nathan, the expert in it all, hadn't given it a second thought. Why would he? Of all the disasters that were happening across America, a limnic eruption was the furthest thing from his mind.

Nathan looked ready. He was suited up in hazmat gear; the oxygen tank weighed a ton but was nowhere near as heavy as the weight of worry on his shoulders.

He had two hours' worth of air, that was it. He rode with the crew into the main portion of town, and then Nathan left them.

As soon as they stopped the vehicles and stepped out, the limnic eruption was the only explanation for what he saw.

Even with the thick mist still in the air, he could see it all.

Bodies strewn across the road, they lay on the sidewalk, in their cars. All of them with the same blueish appearance, enlarged lips, blisters near their mouths, and a frozen expression of fear and pain.

Upon seeing it, Nathan ran. At first to his father's bait shop a block away. The store was still locked tight, and the car wasn't out front.

He then made a beeline straight for his parents' home

His pace slowed down as he neared the home and saw the taillights of his father's car in the driveway. It was still running. He moved closer and saw the back door was open.

"God, no. Please. No. No." He closed his eyes tight and, filled with incredible fear, walked toward the car. He was so focused on the open door, he never saw his father's body in the driveway until his foot hit against him.

He groaned out in pain upon seeing his father and lunged for the car.

With agonizing pain, he cried out from his gut when he saw his daughter strapped in the car seat. He couldn't look, he turned away quickly, unable to stare into the lifeless eyes of his daughter.

Nathan's mother was in the front seat. Her head titled back, mouth wide open.

It had happened shortly after he left.

Why did he leave so early? Why didn't he just stay and die with them?

More than anything he wanted to rip off his headgear and suffocate like they did, join them, but something stopped him, and he didn't.

Nathan undid Gin-Gin's seat restraints and lifted her into his arms. He sobbed from the depths of his soul as he cradled her in his arms.

He didn't know at that moment why he chose to live instead of die. Later on it would come to him. Nathan had to keep going, keep fighting. He had to work to make a difference, a change, at least find a way to predict an event before it happened. If he could save one father from feeling the pain of holding his lifeless child, then his daughter and his parents' death would not be in vain.

PART THREE: THE MISSION

NINE

The simulators did nothing to give Rey an accurate portrayal of the Omni-4. It was breathtaking and huge when she stepped into it the first time, the day before the mission.

It reminded her of an old movie. The world was about to be destroyed by a meteor and a team of misfits were sent into space to divert it. In the movie, the night before the mission seemed ominous and pivotal to those misfits risking their lives.

For the most part, the crew of The Noah Mission weren't misfits, they were capable, experienced people. Rey was the misfit, and not a single member of the crew made her feel that way.

She had the nervousness of the movie crew, the fear, she didn't think she was risking her life. That thought didn't cross her mind until the night before.

The day had been filled with final tidbits of information. More training in the simulator followed by a final magnificent dinner. A tender steak she could cut with a fork, a lobster tail so juicy it melted like butter; Rey felt like a prisoner on death row enjoying her last meal.

Then she stepped for the first time into the Omni-4. It appeared wide on the outside, but interiorly it seemed narrow. It was nowhere near as big as it looked. It reminded her so much of an airplane. Everything about it was like a plane, only, much smaller. Gone were the days of the space suit and heavy helmets, the new craft was designed to eliminate that. After the recognizable nose of the craft, the rest of it was more triangular. A good portion was cargo and the rear sides were thick from the solar panels. The front end was no bigger than an airplane cockpit. Three seats lined up behind each of the two pilot chairs with a thin aisle in the middle. Behind those seats was the kitchen area, similar to the galley on a plane. There was a sleeping area after that, if it could even be called that. The beds were more like shelves, reminding Rey of luggage compartments in a plane, stacked up on top of each other. Rey was told the flight was short and the only time she'd sleep in one of those was if the Noah planet wasn't conducive enough to sustain life. To which Nathan Gale replied, "Then why bother staying?"

But the answer to that was simple. The Noah planet obviously had a sun. The Omni would need to land, eject its solar panels and regenerate the fuel cells for takeoff. The Omni took off much like a plane, but with higher speed, and unlike an airplane was able to penetrate into the mesosphere.

Even the fantastic dinner, the drinks and the long day didn't help Rey feel tired enough to sleep. She found herself putting on her NASA work T-shirt, pants, and sporting a pair of flip flops, then decided to leave the housing building and take a walk.

No one stopped her.

It was pretty busy on base. There were vehicles moving about along with people walking, even at one in the morning. Giant lights in the distance, much like those on a football field, were a guiding point. She knew they were lighting up the area where they were preparing the Omni for the late morning takeoff.

She walked toward the area to watch. They were loading more items into the back of the Omni. Rey stood there for a while until the air felt as if it were chilling.

When she turned around, she heard a voice, almost like a talk radio and saw the open door on one of the hangers. Walking by it, she peeked in and then stopped.

It was astonishing.

The entire hanger looked like a holograph for the solar system, the outlined images seemingly dangled in the air. Nate walked from a table of computers over to the images, and using his hands in a swiping manner, brought the earth into center view. He then zoomed in on the outline of Asia and a pulsing yellow light. He shook his head, then looked left to the sun. When he turned his body he spotted Rey.

"Can I help you?" he asked.

"I'm sorry. I am. I was walking by and I saw ... and I apologize."

"No need. I was just working."

"This is amazing in here," Rey said. "Can I ask what all this is?"

"Sort of like my way of taking it all in. Would you like to come and take a look?"

Rey nodded and followed him in.

Nate walked over and shut off the voice sound bites. It sounded like newscasters but only snippets of the news.

"Interesting choice to listen to," she said.

"That's my selection."

"For?"

"Two weeks ago, I was part of a time capsule program. Before in my life, I thought they were silly. You know, why put stuff in a tube or box and bury it for the future to find? I mean, wouldn't we have history books, internet? Now I find them imperative. One day, someone from the future or even another planet will find the time capsule and know who lived here. How we lived and loved."

"And who Bill Clinton and Ronald Reagan were."

"That ..." He waved his finger. "Was my contribution. I put in soundbites of as many presidents as I could get. The future may not know who or what the presidents were. I think I explained it."

"Strange you didn't put in music," she said.

"I probably would have had I not stopped listening to music two years ago."

"You stopped listening to music? Altogether?"

"I didn't listen on purpose," he replied. "I guess it's silly, but any song, rock, oldies, country, it didn't matter, every single song made me think of the family I lost. No matter what the song, I always heard something in the lyrics, so I stopped listening."

"That makes sense. I'm sorry you lost your family," Rey said.

"I'm sorry you lost yours."

"Thank you." She took a deep breath. "Now, tell me what all this is." She pointed to the planets.

"I wanted to work a little more before we left." Nate walked over to the center of the solar system hologram. "Silly as it sounds, I vowed when my daughter died that I would figure out what is happening to this world and do what I could to stop it. Or at least play a part."

"It doesn't sound silly to me."

"Yeah, well, here I am. Two years later and I'm no closer." He tossed out his hand. "Just when I think I know what's going on, it changes. Just when I think I can predict the next huge event, I can't. None of it makes sense."

"I don't understand," Rey said. "I thought it was just nature saying it's time."

"In a sense that's true. However, nature doesn't work the way it's happening. The world doesn't just wake up one day and say, hey, there's gonna be some devastating changes and in a hundred years it's gonna be a different world. And at the rate it's increasing per day a hundred years is generous. Global changing, continental changing events like this take thousands, tens of thousands of years, not a hundred."

'Maybe ... and I'm not the scientist here, maybe it's been happening and we just didn't notice it."

"I'd say that's true, if it continued on a path. But it hasn't, it's been over the past three years. I mean, we have a population of seven billion plus that's been cut by a billion people." He pointed to the hologram diagram of the earth, spinning it as he spoke. "Earthquakes, sea levels rising, underwater volcanic eruptions that are unprecedented, events like what happened to your family, ten-foot mudslides out of nowhere. Events that took mine. Freshwater lake limnic eruptions. These things had no precedence. Earth isn't in some sort of cycle. I feel it. I just can't prove it."

"What do you mean?"

"I mean something else is causing all this to happen.

That's my theory. The sun, the moon … something … something out there. Every day I look. I stare for hours and every day I come up blank."

"In the solar system?" she asked.

Nate nodded.

"Wouldn't you see it, though? I mean, all the satellites, the space station, this …" She pointed to his hologram display.

"Unfortunately, taking in all that we have out here"—he pointed—"we can only see ten percent of the sky at any time. That's all we can monitor."

Rey snickered.

"What's funny?"

"I don't mean to laugh, but I was just thinking of a movie that said the same thing about monitoring only ten percent of the sky. So you think something out there"—she indicted—"in all this vastness is causing this?"

"I do."

"Well, one good thing: in twelve hours you're gonna get a better look. Maybe you'll see it."

"Maybe," he said looking at his display before he shut it down. "I can only hope."

TEN

Curt tapped his pen from tip to end as he contemplated what he would write. To him it was a special journal entry. The last one before he went on The Noah Mission.

He sat at the desk by the window in his room, sipping on his 'allowed' amount of bourbon. He saw Rey walking away and wondered where she was going in the middle of the night. Then probably figured she was just restless like he was.

Everyone's demeanor was different at dinner. Almost solemn.

When he had that thought it was then he realized what his opening would be.

May 14

I wonder if the feeling at dinner was more nerves, or perhaps some sort of group premonition of something going terribly wrong.

I joke a lot, but I'm scared of this mission. This is the biggest one yet.

Three of our team have only had knowledge of this mission for months. One crew member for only a couple of weeks. Everyone on the team is supposed to pull their weight one way or another. That is how we will complete this with success and safety. I can't figure out what she will contribute. Her knowledge of wormholes is fiction based. She has no other skills other than what we have taught her.

Even with her lack of ability, Finch and I are a strong combination. We have been training for years. Long before the Noah was discovered. We were training when there was no destination planet. In fact, a part of me feels as if I have been training for this mission my entire life.

Each member of the crew has limited or no emotional ties. I, myself, seem to have pushed people away for as long as I can remember. Perhaps my way to ensure no one will miss me or mourn should I not return.

My general concern is that. Not death. We are going to an unknown, unchartered planet. The possibility exists that we may not return. Something about this whole thing feels off. I haven't spoken my concerns out loud, but the worry is there.

He exhaled, leaned back in his chair and lifted his glass. He noticed Finch standing in his doorway, arms folded, staring in what looked like a judgmental way.

"What's up?" Curt asked.

"Your door was open," Finch said.

"Wow, really, I didn't notice," Curt said sarcastically. "What do I owe this middle-of-the-night visit to?"

"You know, you're not supposed to …" He pointed to Curt's drink.

"I'm within my limits."

"Do you know them?"

"Colonel, really?" Curt snapped his chair forward. "What was that about?"

"I know how stressful this is. And given your past and the—"

"Stop." Curt held up his hand. "I'm good. Thank you for your concern. Yes, this is stressful. I'm handling it. Well. Thank you. No worries." He brought his drink to his lips.

"I'm sorry."

"Not a problem." He sipped. "Again, what brings you here, other than to check on my drinking habits?"

"I saw your door open and I just wanted to let you know I ran a check on the cargo. I inspected the cargo and seals. Everything is loaded in."

"Everything?"

Finch nodded.

"Jibs?"

"That's pretty much what most of the cargo is. Curt, I inspected and noticed one of the jibs was a case of bourbon. It said Walt authorized it for you."

"He did. It's in a jib, right? Well, isn't that what the jibs are for. Just in case boxes. If we get stranded, I want that, just in case."

"That makes sense. I'll leave you be. I just wanted to update you. Try to get some rest."

"Colonel."

Finch stopped before leaving. "Yes?"

"I know I wasn't your first choice for this mission as your co-pilot. You make no bones about that. I want you to know, you can be confident in me."

"Curt, listen, we have been working on this mission together for years now. You're right, you weren't my first choice. But you are my partner in this, and I trust you."

"Do you? Because sometimes it seems like you don't and ... that you don't like me much."

"I like you just fine. The only problem I have is that you showboat. You're all about the attention. Sexiest man alive gets ready to save the world but stops to save a woman."

"I don't put myself out there to save people for the attention," Curt said. "I do it so there's one less person that will die in this mess."

"And tomorrow you'll embark on a mission that will hopefully cause millions less people to die in this mess. Enjoy your night cap. Good night."

"Good night." Curt listened to Finch's footsteps fading, and when he knew he was far enough away, he stood, walked to his door and closed it. After that, he returned to what little remained of his drink and to writing in his journal.

NORTH DAKOTA

Tucker Freeman knew something big was on the horizon when the government started buying the land and farms around his place. Tucker never got an offer, probably because he had the biggest barley output in all the dusty prairie.

Of course, at first, no one knew it was the government. Just some people in fancy cars and suits making outrageous offers. Until the checks arrived and they were made out from good old Uncle Sam.

Regis Stone was a bragger. He rushed over to Tucker's place to show him the check.

"Twice as much as my place is worth," Regis said.

"That's a lot of money. What are you gonna do with it?"

"Move to Florida."

And that he did. Regis and his family made a beeline for the sunshine state. That was before half the state was under water. If Regis stood before him now, Tucker would have to ask, "How's that working out for you, ya cocky arrogant bastard?"

Even after everyone moved from their homes, nobody was aware of why the land was needed.

There was lots of speculation, but the only thing that was remotely close to a good guess was when everyone said they were building a mall.

The big giant fences went up and encircled every bit of land they could. Then huge trucks hauled in spotlights.

When groundbreaking began, Tucker was certain it was a mall. It irritated him at first. Why would they build one in the middle of nowhere? Then he started getting angry with the bright lights that lit up the horizon at the end of his property, and the sounds of construction in the middle of the night.

Once Tucker realized what it was, he was excited about it. At forty-two years old, he himself would probably not live to see it serve its purpose, but he was able to watch it being built. It was one of the ARCs that would take people from Earth to a new home.

The large platform was the reason Tucker thought it was a mall, and then they began the ARC. He took pictures every day. After a year, he became a fixture. People knew him, waved to him.

The ARC was not what he imagined. The skeleton of it was as big as nearly two football fields, and eight stories high. The shape of it reminded him of a cruise ship. Only it rounded off on top like a football.

He was told by one of the workers the structure itself would take ten years; that was just the structure, that wasn't factoring in anything else. They hadn't even designed a working and feasible propulsion system.

Watching the ARC was his sunrise and sunset routine. He loved seeing the sun lower behind the structure. It gave him a chance to feel hope for the future in leu of all the disasters and deaths.

"How many people, Pappy?" Nilly, his granddaughter, asked as they sat on the tractor before starting morning chores.

"Ten, fifteen thousand. I don't know," he said.

"Where is it going to go?'

"Up there." He pointed to the sky. "Tomorrow there will be a group of people going into space to check out a planet just like this one. That ship, when it's finished, will take people there too."

"What about the people left behind."

"Well, Nilly Jane, those left behind, they may have it a little easier. Less people, less fighting about food. They hope by the time this goes up, the disasters will have stopped."

"Will you go?" she asked.

"Not me. It's gonna be fifty years. If I am still on this

earth, there won't be room for an old man. You … you'll be just a little older than I am now. You have a chance."

"I won't go," she said folding her arms.

"Why not?"

"This is where I live. I don't want to go somewhere else. I want to stay here. I bet lots of people feel that way."

"You're right. However, honey"—he leaned down and kissed her on the forehead—"people, at this point don't have a choice."

"Will we see the spaceship in the sky today?" Nilly asked.

"We may. Even if we don't we should keep them in our thoughts. Maybe say a prayer."

Nilly nodded and Tucker held her closer. He didn't say any more, he just held her. They'd watch for a little bit more before Tucker began his work day. He would pause during his day to watch the takeoff of the Omni, pause and pray. He knew the crew of needed all the prayers in the world. The fate of mankind depended on it. If they failed, if the planet wasn't habitable, more than likely there wouldn't be such a great second chance to find a new home.

Without a place to go mankind, and a lot of other species, would reach their end at some point in his granddaughter's lifetime.

ELEVEN

In order for the Omni to maneuver into the Androski Worm-hole, they had to approach it just right, at the perfect time of day. Too much sunlight caused the wormhole to be invisible, and the last thing Finch needed was to guide the ship through too close to the edge.

There were theories tossed about that no matter how big the wormhole was, it would crush whatever passed through.

NOAA-13 passed through twice without incident, though it was twenty percent the size of the Omni.

The timing was right, they were ready for takeoff.

The forward fuselage and flight deck were equipped with early warning systems and an ejection pod, so the backup safety of the old-style helmets and suits wasn't necessary.

They were still welcome to wear their suits, though. In fact, Rey decided to do so, but she was the only one. She spent every day practicing how to get in and out of a suit. In the old days it took twenty minutes, now it took ten. It was heavy and bulky, but she wasn't going without one until they left Earth's atmosphere.

She supposed she looked silly and amateurish, much like the time she went on her first cruise with her husband

and wouldn't take off her life jacket ... at all.

"Ma'am," one of the crew told her, "I assure you there is no need for a life jacket at dinner. We are completely safe."

"Yep, and I am sure the folks that ran the Titanic said the same thing. No thank you. I'm good."

She didn't care then and she didn't care now.

She was seated second in the Omni and expected to be leaning back. Instead she was strapped in and felt as if she were taking a plane ride.

Rey was nervous, the whole thing was surreal. Her training was two weeks long as opposed to years with the other crew. Although, she wasn't the only person on the crew that hadn't taken a flight to space. She prayed the ship wouldn't blow up on takeoff or anything else.

There was excitement about seeing the Noah planet, and fear about stepping onto it. Her heart pounded in her chest reverberating up to her ears. Rey shook so badly, and her heart rate was so out of control, that she was given a very mild sedative. To her it felt like she took a couple shots of some very strong alcohol.

She watched and forced a smile when everyone was strapped in. It was nice of NASA to make sure they were secured properly, but what would happen when they took off from the planet to return home. Who would secure them then? The scariest part to Rey was if something would happen to them, no one would know. The only indication that something went wrong was the fact that after two weeks, they never returned.

The door was sealed and her heart dropped to her stomach.

"Can you hear me?" Finch's voice came through her helmet.

"Yes," Rey replied.

"Good. That suit will get warm. Once we make it out of the exosphere, Ben will help you out of it and you'll be much more comfortable for the remainder of the flight."

"Thank you."

"It'll be alright."

Rey took a deep breath. She hated the feeling of hearing her own breathing in her head.

Then before she knew it, it was time.

"Paradise to Omni, you are clear."

"Roger that," Finch replied. "Initiating sequence."

"Ms. Harper," Tom Waite's voice was in her helmet. "Try to relax."

Everyone looked at her.

Did they expect she'd be calm or an expert?

"Godspeed, Omni," Waite said. "You are good to go."

From her seat she couldn't really see much of what Finch or Clutch were doing. Their arms moved about and they went back and forth with words she didn't understand.

"All you," Finch told Clutch.

"Ladies and Gentlemen this is your co-pilot," Curt said as the Omni began to move, mimicking an airplane pilot. "Weather on Noah is unknown at this time. We hope for clear skies. Time of flight to the wormhole, three hours and fifty minutes. Sit back and enjoy the flight."

As the ship moved at incredible speed, Rey felt herself

pressed back against the seat as music played in her helmet.

What was that song?

An old one, a very old one. 'Fox on the Run.'

Everyone groaned. Not Rey. She just had to focus on staying calm and listened to the music, which seemed so fitting for the speed of the occasion.

"You alright?" Ben asked as he removed her helmet.

Rey gasped. "Yes, thank you."

"Let's get you out of this suit. So you can look around and take in the awesomeness."

Rey nodded quickly. She wasn't ready for when he undid her strap. Of course, she knew she'd experience weightlessness. Her stomach already felt it. But the moment she was free from her seat restraints, she floated upward. Which seemed to amuse everyone, because she wasn't ready.

Rey had done really well in simulation, she had to get it together, she had to.

When she first started teaching, she was young, wet behind the ears and the whole feeling was overwhelming that first day ... being on the ship felt the same way.

Until she looked out the window.

She expected to be awed, her breath taken away from the beauty, but instead there was something scary about it. Earth was in the distance and behind them a blackened speckled sky that reeked of infinity. Rey found herself just staring, not moving, not talking.

Sandra made her way to Rey. "You feeling okay? Do you need anything?"

"I'm fine, thank you."

"Amazing, yet scary, huh?" Nate said to her.

"Yeah, yeah it is."

"Let's go explore," he suggested.

He offered his hand as assistance for her, maybe even a guide, but she declined. She needed to do it herself.

The feeling of floating was better than she expected, except no one told her how bubbly her stomach would feel. She had been on the Omni before flight, but it was a completely different experience now.

Everyone had their light duties, things to check, making sure everything was secure. Everyone except Rey.

She felt useless and wondered when she would be of any use on the mission. Although it was clear she was the face of the people, Rey wanted to contribute.

Nate put her to work. He had to check his items in cargo, then the testing utensils he would use once they entered Noah's atmosphere.

"What are you hoping for?" Rey asked.,

"Something close to Earth. I think we'll get that. The water is blue, and the water and green of vegetation tells me there has to be a breathable atmosphere. If there's not, we're gonna be on this ship until we power up enough to return home. And gravity, we need gravity. It's hard to tell from the pictures, but I envision a place very Earth-like."

"And if there is breathable air and gravity?" she asked. "Then what? What do we do for two weeks?"

"Explore. Test the soil, the vegetation, look for the signs of a previous civilization, try to figure out what went wrong.

Why they aren't there. The two weeks will fly by."

"What if there's life still there? What happens then?"

"Hopefully they aren't hostile. Hopefully they don't treat us like an Area 51 experiment."

"That's not funny," she said.

"I'm not joking."

Nate was amazing with her. When they finished checking all his equipment and cargo, both of them familiarized themselves with what the others were doing, then went off to the kitchen.

There were two types of food. One designed to eat in flight, the other once they were situated on The Noah.

Between eating, working, and checking out everything on the ship, the four hours to the Androski flew by and Finch was soon calling them back to their seats.

"Should I suit up?" Rey asked.

"If you want," Finch replied. "At this point. I don't know that it's going to matter."

Rey strapped in as did everyone else.

"There she is," Finch said.

Rey couldn't see it, it looked like nothing. She didn't even know what she was searching for.

"Paradise, this is Omni," Finch said. "We are ready to go through."

"Omni, this is Paradise, you are clear. Last transmission until you return."

"Roger that."

"Godspeed."

"And Roger that, as well."

He was scared, or at least nervous, Rey sensed that. Going through the wormhole caused a quiet in the ship.

"Here we go," Finch announced.

The ship tilted to the right, but didn't pick up speed, he kept it steady.

What would happen? No one had ever gone through a wormhole.

Rey kept repeating in her mind, *The satellite was fine. The satellite was fine. We'll be fine.*

"We're in," Finch stated.

Rey exhaled in relief, but that relief was short-lived.

There were no expectations, but a part of her seemed to think it would be like going through a doorway.

It wasn't. The second they entered the wormhole, flashes of light surrounded them and as she looked out the window, it looked as if space bent. The stars were no longer dots of light, but streaks.

The flashes picked up in intensity, and the entire ship filled with a blinding light before Rey began to feel the pressure on her body.

It felt as if someone was sitting on her chest. The pressure increased and the ability to breathe lessened.

No, no, no, what's happening?

Her head spun and when she turned to look at Nate, it was if she were in a thick pool of mud. Unable to move, think, see.

She blinked hard, trying to focus. Nate was gripping the arm rest of his seat and then his head fell forward.

Rey tried to call out. But her words, "What's happening?" were slurred and deep. Was that even her voice?

She watched as Ben and Sandra passed out. Curt was next. Finch tried to reach for him, then his arm fell.

That was the last thing Rey saw.

The last of her air left, she could no longer inhale or exhale.

At that moment, as they traveled through the wormhole, Rey tried with everything she had to gasp for that one final breath, she couldn't, all she could think was, *This is it. I'm gonna die.*

Her head fell forward, and like everyone else aboard the Omni, she passed out.

TWELVE

With a heaving breath that sounded more like a gasp, Finch snapped his head upward as he found himself suddenly awake and clinging to the air that entered his lungs.

Not only did he find himself conscious, he found the ship guiding on a direct course toward a light blue colored planet that blocked everything in his vision. The planet was huge and covered in a thick, blur cloud formation. It was as if it were blocking the other side of the wormhole, but why didn't the NOAA document it? It was a frightening sight, especially when Finch noticed the speed of their approach.

Finch not only had to clear his head, he had to think quickly.

Within seconds, alarms started blaring.

Curt jumped in his seat as he, too, woke up.

"What the hell?" Curt asked. "What happened?"

"I don't know," Finch answered. "We're being pulled by this planet's gravity and we need to pull out. We don't know what's behind that cloud formation."

"That's not it, is it? That's not The Noah," Curt said.

"No. It's not. I can't see Noah."

Curt helped work the control to take the reins of the Omni about the point everyone else was waking up.

"System is straining," Curt said. "She wants to land."

"We can't," Finch replied. "Nate, you with us? What do we know about this place?'

"Scanning the surface now," Nate said. "Nothing friendly, it would tear us up. The terrain is rough. And cloud coverage would inhibit a clear solar charge."

Ben added, "It would take approximately three weeks to get enough power to lift off. That would be too long."

"There is something we can do," Curt suggested. "We dump everything we have from auxiliary and basically lift off from this planet's pull."

"If we do that," Finch said, "we're pretty much gonna coast our way into the atmosphere of Noah."

"Yeah, but that will leave us enough power to navigate a landing," Curt said.

"Ben?" Finch called him. "What will that do?"

"Suck up all our power. Curt's right. We can land on Noah. We'll just have to charge fully, which will take a week. However, there may be another way. Propel enough to catch the orbit," Ben suggested. "That will stop us from depleting completely."

"Slingshot?" Finch asked.

"Slingshot," Ben replied.

"Then we have no choice, that's what we do," Finch said and looked at Curt. "On my call hit the propulsion."

"Roger that."

"On three ... two ... one ... now!"

The pressure of the thrust pushed Rey against the back of her seat; there wasn't an inch of her body she could move.

Glued there, fingers stuck from seconds earlier when she gripped for dear life.

She gained consciousness at the sound of the alarms and couldn't imagine how Colonel Finch or Captain Henning were thinking so quickly, when she herself was dazed, confused, and scared out of her wits.

She kept her eyes tightly closed, not by choice, but more by a frightened instinct. The voices of the crew, working as a team, flowed from one person to the next, like a well-rehearsed script. In her disordered state of mind, she couldn't decipher who was saying what. They spoke quickly and emotionless, and all sounded the same, even Sandra, as the ship seemed to shake out of control.

"Vitals are good, try to focus on calm. We don't need heart rates right now out of control."

"Engines holding steady. Auxiliary power at seventy percent depletion."

"It's a little hard to focus, right now, I'm trying to get us out of this."

"Ben, where do we need to be when we land on Noah?"

"Jesus, what is this planet?"

"We need to be at fifteen, optimal twenty if we need to search a landing site."

"We can do this."

"Auxiliary power at fifty-five percent."

"Oxygen levels holding steady."

"Forty percent."

"We need more."

"It can't handle more."

"It has to. I need more."

"Thirty-five percent."

"This is its moon."

"What?"

"Why the pull is so great ..."

"Thirty percent."

"We're detaching."

Oh my God, Rey screamed in her mind. *The Omni is breaking apart.*

She was prepared for some sort of explosion. Finch called out, "Clear," and she felt the pressure of the propulsion release and had she not been strapped in, she would have floated forward.

Before she could register what had just happened, slowly and with a sound of shock, Curt said, "Holy shit."

Everyone grew silent, and she felt a tap to her arm. Rey opened her eyes. Nate was trying to get her attention. When he had it, he pointed forward.

Rey leaned to her right and saw instantly why the crew was speechless.

In the distance, clear and beautiful, was Noah.

THIRTEEN

"Damage?" Finch asked.

"We're good," Ben replied. "Other than a few things knocked around."

"Do we know what happened?" Finch questioned.

"Going through the Androski. I don't know ..." Ben shrugged. "We lost all power for about twenty seconds. Oxygen stopped flowing. We passed out. Fortunately, everything came back on."

Rey heard that, but had a hard time processing the scientific information. How could they? Maybe it was their experience in space that caused them to ignore what was out the window. Rey was in awe. Completely awestruck. Her eyes fixated not only to the deep blackness of space, but the huge blue body of mass that they nearly crashed into. As they inched forward her heart beat out of her chest, when the new earth planet, The Noah, came into view. It was breathtaking both figuratively speaking and physically. Rey could not catch her breath.

A cluster of emotions hit her, most of which, she wanted to cry. It was overwhelming and there would never be another moment like it in her entire life.

Words could not describe it.

"Right, Rey?" Finch tapped her shoulder.

"I'm sorry what? I can't stop looking out this window."

Finch smiled gently. "That's fine. It's an amazing view. I was just talking about how we lost oxygen, and you wanted to wear the suit. We urged you not to."

Rey mumbled, her eyes never straying from the view. "I should have worn my suit."

"Then what?" Nate asked her. "The rest of us weren't. We would have passed out and you would have been awake. What if it never came back on? You would have been aware and alive when this thing crashed into that planet. Me, personally, I wouldn't want to see it coming."

Curt turned his seat to face Nate. "Is it a planet or a moon of Noah?"

"It's too big to be a moon," Nate answered. "But it does orbit Noah, from what we can see."

"Looks like there's another moon as well." Curt pointed. "Two moons. That one's further."

Finch swiped his forefinger over his top lip as he stared outward toward Noah. "Estimated time until arrival?"

Ben answered, "Three hours, six minutes; we are on the dark side now. Which is the water side. We want to aim for the large land mass."

"Three hours," Nate said. "Puts the blue moon about two hundred thousand miles away from Noah. Which is about a hundred thousand miles closer than our moon. That explains the wide coastlines. High tide has to be massive and dangerous. Our moon controls the tides. Imagine what that blue thing does to the water on Noah."

"Blue thing," Curt chuckled, then turned serious. "You

know what's really awesome? We get to name them. We're the explorers here. We get to give the names. We should give them something cool."

"For now, we can just stick to blue moon and white," Finch said. "At least it looks that way."

"Boring," Curt added.

"This is amazing," Finch spoke in awe. "I mean ... it's so much like Earth."

"We are not alone," Sandra stated. "We always knew there were other planets like Earth out there. We just needed to find them."

"It could be one of dozens of exoplanets found with the right photosynthesis," Nate said. "Trappist System ... or better yet, this could be Kepler 452B. It's in a habitable zone. Conditions right for liquid water ..." He pointed at Noah as example. "It's about fourteen hundred light years away from Earth. The ESI or Earth Similarity Index point eighty-three. Which means eighty-three percent of it matches Earth. It's terrestrial, and green is vegetation, which typically means oxygen."

"It's obviously not tidal locked," Ben added. "At least we don't think so."

"What does that mean?" asked Rey.

"Means it's like Earth's moon. One side of the moon always faces Earth. A lot of those Kepler type planets were tidal locked. One side always faced the sun. With any exoplanets it is hard to determine if there is a magnetic field like Earth. Which is needed to protect it from the sun."

"And ..." Nate added. "Does it have an atmosphere, and is it conducive to light?"

Finch faced the team. "We can talk, we can educate each other until the blue moon rises and falls. But whether we can breathe the air, drown from the skies, walk on the soil, or fry up from radiation are all irrelevant, because it's not going to matter if that planet is hostile to life or not. We don't have a choice in the matter," he said. "In three hours ... we land."

PART FOUR: THE ARRIVAL

FOURTEEN

The primary body of land on Noah was an easy target. Nate estimated its landmass to be close to fourteen million square miles. Curt joked that they should 'aim for the middle' when looking for a place to land.

It wasn't a matter of aiming. The landing site had to be perfect. An area long and flat for landing and takeoff, plus optimal exposure to sunlight.

The northern most part of the landmass was white, indicating ice, so Finch set a course for the eastern coast, south of the frozen tundra, and while close to the coastal area, far enough inland to be clear from what Nate believed would be dangerous tides.

Taking a page from Rey's paranoid book, they all suited up for the landing.

They knew the second they began the decent the planet had an atmosphere, though what it consisted of remained to be seen.

The entry was smooth, with Finch switching to airplane mode to find a feasible landing spot. It depleted most of their power, leaving them moments away from a powerless landing.

Finch wanted to land in a desert area which was twenty

miles south from their resting spot. That wasn't feasible given the power situation.

They landed in an area that was sandwiched between a wide beach and rolling green hills covered in plants and trees. Though flat, the surface was littered with large rocks that weren't seen from the air.

It was a rough and bumpy landing.

Rey bounced in her seat so hard, she got an instant headache. She swore then and there, never again would she travel in space. Not that she'd get the chance.

She expected excitement and enthusiasm when they landed, instead, everyone was silent, taking a moment to catch their breath.

Finch was the first to take off his helmet. He inhaled then nodded to Curt. "Internal life support?"

Curt reached up to his controls. "Initiated."

"Solar panels."

Curt pressed a few more buttons. "Deployed and charging."

"Oh, yeah," Ben said through the helmet speaker. "We definitely have gravity."

"What is it?" Nate asked.

"Give me a second." Ben undid his helmet and lifted it off. After undoing his belt he stood. "Yep, we have gravity." He walked to his work station behind the seats.

Rey didn't need a scientist to announce they had gravity. She felt it. Her stomach felt weird and every part of her body seemed to experience the blood moving through every fiber of her muscles. She removed her helmet when she saw

Nate do the same and listened to the shop talk between them. Here they went again. All doing their jobs and Rey had nothing. She had none. Yes, she was given a crash course for everyone else's job, but she was like the understudy in a play. Waiting in the wings for something to happen.

"Dr. Gale," Finch called him. "I need a reading."

"Right away, Colonel." Nate stood and like Ben went to his work station.

"Dr. Anderson, prepare medical," Finch ordered.

"Right away, Colonel," Sandra replied.

"Curt, life?" Finch asked.

Curt shook his head. "Nothing. At least not here."

"What's our gravity, Ben?"

"Eight point seven Gs," Ben announced. "Pretty damn close to Earth's nine point two."

"I always wanted to be a little lighter on my feet," Finch joked. "Dr. Gale?"

"Oh my God," Nate said.

"What?"

"Air sample is in," Nate replied. "We have an amazing cocktail of oxygen, nitrogen, methane, carbon monoxide, and argon."

"But is it the right cocktail?" Finch asked.

"It's the perfect cocktail."

"Breathable air?"

"Breathable air."

Finch, in a rare show of excitement, clenched his fist

and drew it in. "Yes." He stood and began to remove his suit. "What are the surface conditions?"

"It's windy," Nate answered. "Might be the norm. Might not. Right now it's reading ten miles per hour with twenty mile gusts. Temperature … seventy-three degrees."

"Wait. What? The surface temperature is seventy-three?" Finch asked.

"Couldn't be more perfect."

"So there's no reason we can't just walk out there?"

"No reason."

"Alright team," Finch announced. "I don't see why we all can't be the Neil Armstrong here." He walked down the aisle past Rey and to the back, speaking as he did. "One small step for man, one giant for the survival of humanity. I'm excited, I know you are. Let's take off the suits and head out." He handed Rey a baseball-style cap, but it didn't have a rim.

"What is this?" she asked.

"I figured you should have the honor of recording all this. Camera's on the top." He showed her. "This button here starts it. Will you?"

"Absolutely." Rey took the cap and adjusted it to fit her head.

FIFTEEN

From the second they stepped foot onto the planet it was, *Now what?*

Before that first step, air samples were taken once more. Rey was given the honor of being the second one out of the Omni, directly behind Finch. She turned on the camera keeping her head tilted up to capture as much as she could of his expression.

"Home?" Finch said as he stepped from the Omni. "It could be."

Rey was nervous when she took the first step. It was solid ground. Everyone's expression was that of being amazed, happy ... excited.

But that was short-lived.

At least for Rey.

Her mind went to, *Now what?*

No one really mentioned a plan after landing, as if they never expected it to be viable. Nothing was discussed about what they did once they left the ship. They spoke about remaining on the ship until the cells were recharged. How they'd live in close quarters until they could lift off again and return home.

But there they were, and they pretty much just stood

111

there.

Would they perch a flag?

Rey reached up and shut off the camera, not really sure what she should video document.

"First order of business," Finch said. "We have two weeks here. Our bodies are still on Earth time." He looked at his watch. "And to us it is seven o'clock. Let's unpack, get our gear, and set up camp for the night. We'll begin exploration in the morning. If you venture anywhere, do so in pairs and not far. We have work. We might as well get started now."

The team seemed eager; Rey didn't know what to do or where to start. She followed Finch back into the Omni.

"Pretty amazing, isn't it?" Finch asked.

"I really don't know how to take it. It's just hard to believe we're not even in the same solar system," Rey said.

"I think as we explore, we'll learn a lot."

"Can I ask you a question?"

"Sure."

"What am I supposed to do? I mean, everyone seemed to just click into gear. I feel like a third wheel."

"You shouldn't. Document." He touched her cap. "Talk to them. Everything we do here, people back home will want to know. Ask questions. Walk outside, look around. But don't forget to give that camera to Ben to charge."

"Sounds good." Rey reached up and turned on the camera. "Okay Colonel Finch. You're on. What is your job right now?"

"Right now, I am in charge of unloading supplies.

Tracking what is done, but mainly preparing and charging the rover for expedition."

"The rover is?"

"A manned vehicle we will take. It's a pretty big hunk of land. We'll take in as much as we can on ground."

Rey thanked him. It wasn't much of an interview, but a start. She followed him to the back of the ship and to the cargo area, where Curt was waiting by the open hatch.

"Hey." Curt wore a backwards baseball cap, making him look much younger than he was. "You're our historian, I see."

"I guess," she said. "So, what are you up to?"

"Me. I have to help Finch unload, and I am in charge of setting up our camp for the night."

"Sounds pretty simple." She looked left to right. "Where is the rover?"

Hands on hips, Curt smiled again. "In about eight different crates right now."

"It needs to be built? Are you doing that?"

"Nope." Curt pointed to Ben who was opening a case. "He is."

Rey stepped down the ramp of the hatch and intended on talking to Curt, but she saw Nate who moved a computer tablet around as if he were aiming it.

She took a few steps his way and that was when she finally looked around.

They had landed in a dirt and rock area that stretched for as far as she could see. It was narrow though, with grassy like areas on both sides. To the right and left of the grass were rows of trees.

"Pilgrims," Nate said catching her attention.

"I'm sorry, what was that?" she asked.

He stood next to her. "When we arrived here, I imagined this was how the pilgrims felt. First on a new land. Uncharted. Untouched. The first people to be there."

"Only they weren't."

"No, they weren't," Nate said.

"The natives?"

"Could be anywhere. This is a large landmass."

"So you think there is life here?" she asked.

"I'll be surprised if there isn't. Do you mind?" He reached for her cap.

"You want me to turn it off?"

"Yeah, could you. I just would rather not be recorded until I have factual information."

"Sure." She reached and turned off the camera.

"I promise to let you film when I do."

"What are you doing now?"

"Looking around mainly. First order was to set up my sundial." He pointed to a rod near the rear of the ship. "I need to know how long the days are. I figure by my watch, I'll be able to track, very primitively, how long the days are. Walk with me?" he asked. "We're supposed to be in pairs."

"Sure. Where are we going?"

"Exploring the area. Not too far though. I want to compare." He lifted his tablet.

"What do you think?"

"I think this is a twilight zone world. The trees around us. They look like a hybrid of what we have on Earth. A hybrid between a larch and hemlock trees. I mean they are both part of the Pinaceae family, but still. How is that possible?"

"How is what possible, the hybrid? Maybe it's not a hybrid. Maybe it's just this world's trees and they look like what we know as a hemlock and larch."

"That's a point."

"Or the Frontier crashed here."

He paused in walking. "The Frontier."

"Yeah, you know it was launched seventy or so years ago ..."

"I know about the Frontier. I just ... why do you say that?"

"It had seedlings, recordings, a time capsule for space," she said. "Much like the one you contributed to, I guess. Well it was sent into space. They stopped tracking it. What if it crashed here. Farfetched I know, but if it went through the Androski and crashed here, it could have inadvertently ..."

"Terraformed."

Rey snapped her finger. "Yes. That. But that takes a while."

"With two moons, it's more than likely the rotation is faster, anything is possible."

"We'll be here for two weeks. I bet you're excited about the things you'll see."

Nate continued walking. "I am. I'm more excited about

115

the possibility of life here or the previous civilization."

"And you're sure there was one?"

"With ninety percent certainty. Things I saw on the satellite indicated that. And if I'm right, it's not far from where we are. Something big wiped out life here. And I think it was fast. This planet has a lot of hostilities. For example ..." He showed her the tablet. "Here is a picture I took from the Omni. The land mass where we landed. We're here ... from my estimate. South of the frozen zone." Using his fingers he zoomed in on the picture."

"How can you tell?"

"Our landing strip. It's bare. No life. It extends hundreds of miles. This is it." He pointed to the image.

Amongst the green, the brown line looked like a road from the Omni image.

"There's a reason no life grows there," he said. "It could be an active fault line."

"An active fault line?"

"Something like that. It has to be something that happens over and over that prohibits growth."

"Sounds dangerous," Rey said.

"It could be. If only ..."

Both Rey and Nate turned their heads slowly to the loud sound. A whooshing sound that grew louder.

"Sounds like the ocean," Rey shouted over the noise.

"Yeah, it does."

"I thought we landed twenty miles inland."

"That's what we calculated."

"Has to be wrong. How can we hear an ocean from twenty miles away?"

"We can't. It sounds like an ocean. But have you ever heard one that loud?"

"Not even from the beach."

Nate grabbed hold of her wrist and began to move quickly, almost running toward the sound, dragging her along.

"Should we be headed this far?" Rey asked.

Nate didn't verbally reply. He kept pulling her.

The sound was deep and barreling, growing louder and louder. While it sounded like an ocean, it lacked the noise of crashing waves, only a pulsing, roaring sound.

They ran through the deep tree area and all Rey kept thinking was they were never making their way back. Nate ran aimlessly, not paying attention to where they were going.

Yelling for him to stop was impossible, the sound was so loud.

Five minutes into the run, the temperature made a sudden drop and the trees bent inland as a steady wind gust pushed against them.

She kept thinking, *This can't be safe, this can't possibly be safe*. With each step they moved, the wind beat harder at them and they fought the force against monsoon-strength winds. Her eyes fought to stay open.

"What are we doing!" Rey shouted.

"What?"

Of course he didn't hear her, she could barely hear

herself. She was almost afraid of him letting go, for fear she would turn into some sort of Dorothy from *Wizard of Oz* and get swept away.

Suddenly the shading from the trees changed and the brightness of the planet's sun blasted them. They were nearing the edge of the woods.

Still clutching her wrist, Nate came to an abrupt halt then shot out his arm to hold her back like a parent holding back a child in the front seat when the vehicle stops abruptly. Rey's own arm along with Nate's was against her chest and she still tipped forward. It was as if the world had dropped off. Had it not been for the wind pushing against them, they surely would have fallen.

She caught through her peripheral vision Nate reaching up for her cap. He was turning on the camera.

After inching back, Rey's focus was down. She couldn't help it. Even though scared, a part of her was in awe at the distance between her feet and the earth over three hundred feet below her. At the base of the cliff was a beach. Not the type she was used to seeing on vacation or in pictures, more unchartered, untouched. Littered with seaweed and other things dragged in from the ocean.

Nate lifted her chin to get her to look forward.

The beach extended outward for miles and the ocean was barely seen on the horizon as it blended with the sky.

Why was it so loud?

Then it grew even louder. Rey flinched from the noise, but the sight of it in the distance made her squint. Was it an optical illusion or was the ocean growing?

It had to be an illusion, she was miles away from the

water.

Both her and Nate didn't move. Within thirty seconds she realized her eyes weren't playing tricks. The swelling of the ocean was real and not only was it increasing in size it was moving at incredible speed their way.

Rey took a step back.

"Look at the size of that thing!" Nate shouted in her ear. "It has to be at least a hundred meters high."

"Bigger," she said as she moved back some more.

"We're fine! It can't get us way up here. It will break when it hits the shore! I want this on film! The others won't believe it!"

Had Rey not seen it, she wouldn't have believed it either. The giant wave was huge and it wasn't the only one. Directly behind it, just like any normal tide was another one rolling in, and behind those, another formed. It wasn't a freak storm, it was a normal occurrence.

It grew bigger as it moved to the shore, but unlike Nate said, that wave wasn't showing any signs of breaking.

When the monstrous wall of water connected with the beach and kept coming, Rey echoed Nate's sentiments of "Oh, shit!" and they had the same instincts at the same time. They spun and ran as fast as they could in the opposite direction of the cliff.

The feeling wasn't there when she walked, but Rey felt it when she ran. The lower gravity along with the wind gave her near super speed. It was like being in a dream, being able to run incredibly fast without losing her breath. The wind aided her and when she leapt over a fallen tree, the wind took her a good ten feet. Had she not felt so frightened she would have loved the feeling.

The wave was close and she knew it, she could feel the pressure on her back along with the temperature change.

Never was she a fast runner, but there she was, far ahead of Nate. She hadn't a clue if she was even running in the right direction until she saw the others headed their way.

"Go! Turn around!" she shouted.

"Run," Nate yelled.

They didn't move, they just stood there as if Rey and Nate were yelling in some sort of foreign language.

Actions spoke louder than words. That applied both ways. She saw the expression on their faces, especially Finch. He widened his eyes, jolted in surprise and turned quickly.

That was all she saw. Rey was still running when it felt like she was hit by a two by four on the back of her knees. She was moving so fast, the force of the water swept her off her feet and up in the air. She crashed back down and moved along with the heavy current of the water without hitting the ground first.

She rolled in a tumble, then spun clockwise, her body was a raft on a raging rapid. She kept her eyes open trying to maneuver out of the way when she saw herself on a collision course.

Rey was on nature's own Slip and Slide, but it wasn't fun.

She watched the others fall and get pulled down. Perhaps it was the fact she was running, Rey didn't know, but she was carried faster and further than the others. Just as she passed them she watched Ben move with the rushing water, flip upward and slam into a tree.

Watching that made her think of Canonsburg. As she moved out of control, she thought of her family and how they had been swept away in the force of the flash flood.

I can drown. I can hit into a tree. As long as I die, I'm okay with that, she thought and instantly wasn't scared anymore.

There was no stopping it, no controlling it, Rey just rode it out. At the final edge of the woods, the wave broke, rolling her onto the grass.

Nate tumbled after her and Rey stumbled, trying to stand. She was dizzy, her head spun, and she couldn't catch her balance.

Ben, she thought, then yelled to Nate. "Ben." She didn't know if the others saw him or not, but she did. She raced back in that direction, only to make it twenty feet, before another blast of water knocked her back down. That one, not as strong as the previous, brought her to her knees. She stood again and charged forward.

Another thirty feet, she not only saw a third wave, but it carried Ben's body, flopping it around like a puppet.

Perhaps she was inspired by all the stories regarding Curt Henning or maybe just instinct, Rey dove headfirst toward the rushing water and grabbed on to Ben's legs just as he moved by her.

Her weight, holding him, stopped their momentum and she finally realized she was out of breath.

Breathing heavily she crawled on hands and knees to his head. He lay face down and Rey rolled him over. His eyes were closed, his head, face and chest covered in blood. She couldn't determine through his wet clothes where he was bleeding from.

Shaking, she reached for his neck to feel for a pulse. She thought she felt one, but he was out.

"Ben," she called him. "Ben."

Nothing.

In the woods, kneeling by Ben, Rey looked left, right and all around.

She didn't see anyone. Where were they?

"Help!" she cried out. "Help!" Her voice carried through the woods, the rushing sound of ocean had ceased.

Then she saw Nate stumbling her way. Once he spotted her, he picked up speed.

"Is he?" Nate asked.

Rey shook her head. "He's hurt bad."

"Okay, we have to move him and fast," Nate said. "I'll go find the others. Stay here."

Rey nodded and nervously watched Ben.

They had to hurry, she knew that. Even though the freak waves had stopped, they couldn't assume it was over. It was likely more would come and they'd have to find a place that was safe. The problem was, they were in a new land, a new world. They had no idea *what* was considered safe.

SIXTEEN

It took the last of the Omni's power in order for Finch to move the ship just a little more inland so as not to take a chance on any massive waves. Only a little. He'd barely moved it from the dirt section when the ship petered out. The only thing running was the unit used to keep their food cool.

No computers, no lights: for those they'd have to wait until the solar generator had charged for twelve hours.

Even if the ship's internal power was a hundred percent, the sleeping area wasn't conducive for Ben.

Sandra erected the small medical tent, something she expressed that she didn't think she'd need. She set it up at the end of the cargo ramp, so she could easily go in and out of the ship if need be.

"How is he?" Finch asked upon entering the tent. Ben was on a cot hooked up to an IV and a monitor. His head and chest were bandaged, and Sandra stood next to him.

Sandra slowly shook her head. "He's not good. If we were home, it would be a different story."

"What's happening?'

"Without an X-ray it's hard for me to tell. I can guess."

"Please do."

"Fractured eye socket, fractured sternum, punctured

123

lung and there's fluid in there. I'm going to guess it's blood. I inserted a chest tube. He has a severe concussion, but not from striking his head, more so from whiplash. I'm at a loss. He's bad, Finch." She grunted and shook her head. "He isn't going to make if we don't get him home."

"That's not going to happen anytime soon. Going home, I mean. You have him stable, right? What does he need that you can't give him? Does he need blood? Maybe one of us can help. I'm not a doctor, you are. I have no experience whatsoever in medicine, but all those things you mentioned, what is the treatment?"

"Rest, fluids …"

"Can't you give him that?"

"You're frustrating me," she said. "I can't see inside of him to know if anything is wrong. If there is internal damage or not. That … not the fractures, is what will kill him."

"And there's no way to know if he has any internal injuries other than X-rays?"

"Well," Sandra stammered her words some. "There are ways to monitor, signs to watch for."

"Then I suggest you watch for them." Finch held up his hand. "I'm not telling you how to do your job, I don't mean to be a dick. I'm just telling you the options you need … we don't have and they aren't feasible, such as going home. So do what you can … be hopeful. We're in a situation right now where we have to make do. Make do, Doctor, don't give up on him yet."

Finch give her a nod, trying to convey confidence, then after looking down to Ben, he walked from the tent to continue his work.

Rey watched the first of the two moons make an appearance in the sky. It was strange to her, she was used to Earth's moon being small in the sky, the size of a coin. Instead, the first moon, not as bright as the smaller one, was beautiful and blue. It was frightening as well. Instead of looking at a coin-sized planet, she stared at one the size of a saucer.

It really didn't hit until that moment that she was somewhere else. How far away from Earth she was, from the world she grew up in.

The sky was always scary to her. It was mind-boggling to think of the stars and planets around them. Now there she was, on a planet revolving around one of those stars that used to flicker in the sky above her.

It wasn't long after the rush of water that it got dark. There was no typical setting sun that added an orange glow to things. No gradual darkening sky. Instead it was almost like a shadow was cast over them and within thirty minutes the sky darkened and the temperature dropped.

She didn't ask permission to light a fire, after all, they were there to assess whether the planet could sustain human life.

Heat and warmth were one of those things, the other was water. She wondered about fresh water. How would it be determined?

The heating device for the meals was unusable at least for the rest of the evening, but Rey found a piece of wire similar to a hanger. She asked Finch if she could have it, and he told her she could, never asking why.

With it she made a little grate to hold her foil pouch and propped it near the fire, turning it every couple minutes.

Her hands ached. They weren't broken but they were bruised and brush burned. She squeezed them open and shut. The little first aid kit was next to her, but she hadn't opened it yet. She felt silly for wanting to dress her wounds when Ben was clinging to life.

She thought back to that moment, she kept replaying it in her mind, the second he smacked into the tree. It was like his body folded in half then bounced off.

Everything happened so fast, but as she tried to recall the details, the only person she remembered was Ben.

When the water stopped and he was within her hold, she screamed for help. Nate arrived, told her to watch him and then just took off. It seemed like forever before the others arrived, and when they did, she moved out of the way.

They all gathered around to help Ben. All she could do was step back and watch. Just like now, all she could do was sit there.

As much as she wanted to be, or they told her she was, Rey was far removed and not a part of the group.

It hadn't even been twenty-four hours and Rey just wanted to go home. She may not have had a family, or anyone to welcome her when she walked in the door, but it was home and not some alien planet which seemed in the first hour to want to defeat them like an invading germ.

The water was the first day, and she feared what would come next.

It was guilt. Curt recognized the feeling. It had been a while since he felt not only guilty, but felt bad. He had inflated his tent for the evening, set up his quarters, and had gone to the ship for his dinner when he saw Rey.

That was the moment he realized in the weeks that he had known her, he had barely spoken to her. He did when he first met her, and whenever he had to ask her a question, but other than that, he didn't go out of his way to strike up a conversation. Had anyone other than Nate?

It wasn't that he was snobbish or anything like that, he just never really felt the need to talk to her. Until he saw her sitting alone by the fire.

That's when it all hit him.

She picked her packaged food from some contraption in the fire, tossed it back and forth because it was hot, then set it aside and began placing Band-Aids on her wounds.

He didn't see a tent or anything. She was the only one who'd built a fire as well. Did she not realize that she didn't need to?

It was right then that Curt wondered if anyone had talked to her after they arrived. She was running around with that camera cap, they all appeased her. After she walked off with Nate and the water came, that was it. He didn't recall even seeing her. It was as if, at least to Curt, that she wasn't there.

Yet, it was Rey who physically stopped Ben from further injury. She was the one calling out for help, and Curt was just as guilty of pushing her aside for the sake of his team member.

He looked down to his watch. According to earth time it was ten o'clock. It felt much later on this planet.

Seeing her made Curt think of the ninth grade and Kyle Logan. Kyle was the new kid in school and for the first week he sat alone at lunch, no one bothered him. After that week, the other kids started labeling him weird, because they didn't know him.

Curt never took the initiative to get to know Kyle. It was his loss. Kyle went on to make friends and ended up being the all-American everything in school.

He didn't take the step then, he would take the step now.

After getting what he needed from his tent, he walked over to Rey.

He stood above her for a good ten seconds. She never acknowledged him. Either she didn't care to or she was so lost in her thoughts.

"I owe you ..." Curt said, "a huge apology and I'd like to buy you a drink over dinner."

She stared at the fire. "I don't know why you feel the need to apologize. As far as a drink, I haven't seen any bars around."

Curt dangled a bottle before her eyes.

She looked up at him. "You brought that?"

"I did. Share your fire?"

"Sure."

Curt set down the bottle then sat down next to her. In his other hand he held two plastic glasses, and his dinner pouch was under his arm. After he extended the glasses to her, he pulled out the pouch. "Now, how does your heating contraption work?"

"Not very well and not very evenly." She handed him the grate she made. The end of it was shaped into a V that the pouch sat in. "Put it in there and put it in the fire."

"Ah." Curt maneuvered his food pouch in there. "Thank you."

"And I'll take that drink now."

"My pleasure." Curt uncapped the bottle and poured some in a glass for her.

"So why the apology?" she asked.

"I haven't spoken to you, I haven't asked if you're okay, and I haven't thanked you for what you did for Ben."

Rey shrugged. "As far as for Ben, I wasn't thinking. I just did, you know. Talking to me? That's okay. No one really does. And I'm fine, thank you. A few cuts and bruises ... this"—she held up the drink—"will help."

"I aim to please. So ... physically you're okay. What about emotionally? Mentally?"

"I feel a little lost."

"We all do."

"You all have each other."

"We do. And you're part of that. I'm sorry we haven't made you feel that way."

"It's not your job to be my friend. And, I'm going to apologize. I'm coming across really bitchy."

"No, you're not." He held his glass to hers. "Cheers to a new world."

"A dangerous one." She touched glasses with his and took a sip. "Thank you for this. I can't believe you brought a bottle."

"Case."

She coughed. "Excuse me?"

"Oh, I brought a case. See … there is an entire section of cargo called the jibs. Just … in case boxes."

"Just in case?"

"In case we get stuck here. In case we're delayed. Just … in case."

"And the booze is for long term."

"A case won't last that long. I'll ration it, but who knows."

"Good thinking."

Curt smiled and shook his head. "It's the alcoholic in me thinking. Not essentially good thinking."

"You're joking."

"Nope. I am an alcoholic. Now …" He lifted his glass. "I'm okay. I'm controlling it. A couple of years ago, I wasn't. I was bad. I was really bad."

"Was there a catalyst to it?" she asked.

"Nope. Just started really relying on it. I got off of the stuff. Was sober for nearly a year. I fell off the wagon when I realized the world was going to end. However, I am in control of it. I really am. Some people …" He lifted his eyes to Finch who walked across camp. "Don't believe it. But I am."

"If we get stuck on this planet, you'll be back on that wagon."

"After my case is gone."

"Of course," Rey said. "And … you need to turn your food pouch."

"Oops. Thanks." He reached and rotated his food. "So, um, why is your camp not set up?"

"My camp? You mean my box." She pointed to a square fabric case. "I have no idea what's in there. My name is on it. There're no instructions and that wasn't included in my training. I learned how to fire up the ship, even sort of fly it. How to fix a few things. But not how to unpack that camp box. Finch handed it to me. I tried to move it. It's freaking heavy."

Curt laughed. "It's close to fifty pounds. That little black box on the outside of it is your compressor. It inflates and deflates. It has everything in there. Tent, cot, light."

"No instructions."

"You're right. No instructions. How about this? After we eat, I'll teach you how to set it up. You need to get some sleep tonight. Because I'm pretty sure … Captain Adventure over there"—he pointed to Nate who was walking with a lantern into the woods—"is going to have us on the road."

"I would very much appreciate that."

"Great. Then that's what we'll do." Curt reached for his food pouch and brought it toward him. As he lifted his drink to his lips, he spotted Finch staring his way. He swore. Finch watched him in a judgmental way. That irritated him. Keeping eye contact with Finch, Curt finished his drink, as if some sort of defiant demonstration, then returned to his conversation with Rey.

Aside from Sandra, who tended to Ben, Dr. Nathan Gale was working. Finch could see that. Nate never stopped moving. He had set up his tent, a table outside, two lights, and his tablet. He worked there for a while and then he simply disappeared into the wooded area.

Was he nuts?

Gale grabbed his equipment, tucked it under his arm and with a light in hand walked into the woods.

Finch gave him a few minutes, then keeping his distance, followed him not only out of curiosity, but for safety's sake.

"Good evening," Finch called out, announcing his presence as he made his way to Gale, who wasn't far from the edge of the cliff. "What did I say about going out in pairs?"

"Sorry." He lifted his shoulders.

Finch walked toward the cliff's edge. The ocean didn't roar like it had in the day, but it was still loud and a cool breeze was steady. The moons were bright and lit up the fierce body of water. No longer was there a beach below, the water moved into the cliff, crashing its waves against it.

"Holy God, look at this."

"Rose about a hundred and fifty feet, I suppose," Nate said. "How is Ben?"

"Stable. Not out of the woods, I'm afraid."

"Do we have what is needed to provide care?"

"Not everything," Finch said. "But Sandra is doing her best."

"I believe that."

"And ... speaking of working ... how are you?"

"Working." Nate forced a smile. "Everything right now, everything I come up with is pure speculation. I won't have anything concrete for a couple days. I have to study data."

"And that is?"

"Right now, the soil. One of our jobs is to determine if things can grow. Which they can, obviously." He indicated to the trees. "Except on the dead strip."

"The dead strip."

"The dry dirt and rock area where we landed. We landed in a hundred-foot section, but I suspect it's wider in some spots. According to the satellite pictures and the ones I took on approach, this strip goes south another thousand miles and north until it hits the tundra."

"Do you have any indication why it's dirt."

"Yeah, it's a thrust fault. Laymen definition is a crack in the crust."

"That's a huge fault."

"Yeah it is. It also contains quantities of manganese nodules, phosphorites, and metal deposits."

"Okay," Finch sung the word showing his confusion. "This is different how from where we stand?"

"The balance of minerals. Plus, I believe there is a lot of seismic activity in the fault, which stops a lot of growth. Sort of if you park your car in the same spot in the grass all summer. All of this is important. This instrument here ..." He lifted the tool that looked like a hand drill. He pulled a faux demonstration holding it over a tube in the ground. "This probe is designed to prevent contamination."

"I don't understand."

"We don't want to pull anything from the surface into the sample because it won't give us a good look at how long ago whatever happened, happened."

"How far down does it go?"

"It's a NASA thing, a hundred feet. Maybe more."

"So about a third of our cliff?" Finch asked.

"Yep. And that cliff and my samples all kind of go hand and hand with what I am thinking."

"Which is?"

"That it's not a cliff."

Finch cocked back a little and blinked. "Not a cliff."

"I believe it is a continental shelf."

"Why does that sound familiar?"

"Ever go to the ocean and it just goes from deep to really deep?" He waited for Finch to nod. "Well that's the shelf. It drops drastically. Continental shelf."

"Our cliff is something you'd see in an ocean?"

Nate nodded. "At one point this entire area was under water. And the craziest part is … it wasn't that long ago.

IN THE CLUTCH – CURT'S JOURNAL

May 17

We did it.

We landed.

A part of me was fearful that when we went through the Androski we would sail into open space, nothing in front of us and the Noah not even seen.

There she was. A big beautiful planet.

That was, of course, after her moon nearly swallowed us alive.

We used all of our power resources to escape the gravitational pull of the moon, and with just enough power to land on Noah.

Upon arrival, my first thought was the word virgin. The planet had never been harvested, never seen a life-form other than vegetation. It seemed untouched and new.

Something felt off to me. I felt unwelcomed.

Sure enough, the planet tried to wash us off the surface. It could have been that we placed ourselves in harm's way. That bad luck had us landing in the wrong spot. But I genuinely felt the planet didn't want us.

I can't see or sense the advanced civilization that Dr. Gale insists was here.

Although I am no expert, surely there would be traces of a civilized world. Unless it is buried beneath thousands of years of dirt and rock, I don't believe it's here.

We are the first intelligent life force to step foot on this planet.

I believe that.

However, it remains to be seen. This was only the first day. We have a lot more exploring to do.

SEVENTEEN

It was a positive start to a new day.

Power had been restored to the Omni enough for coffee, and Ben groaned in pain, indicating he had regained consciousness. Then he was propped up at his request and moved to the area where everyone had gathered for breakfast.

"Another three or four hours …" Finch looked up to the sky. "Omni will be functional."

"For how long?" Sandra asked.

"Depends," Curt answered. "If we power her up, an hour or so. Then it's back to square one."

"When can we lift off?" Sandra asked.

"Four days," Ben groaned out. "Give it four days."

"Then we can get you home," Sandra said.

"I'm fine."

"Four days is not enough," Nate said. "Not at all. We need to not only test the soil more inland, we need to determine the other hazardous conditions of this planet."

"Ben needs to get home," Sandra insisted.

"I'm fine," Ben said.

"Yeah, right," Sandra snapped. "You aren't, and we can

do what we can, but when they send a terraform team here and colonists, they'll learn all they can. Ben's health is more important."

"I'm fine," Ben repeated. "Another day I'll be walking around."

"See." Curt pointed at him. "That's one tough guy. So, here's my question, Nate. You told us this entire area was under water not long ago."

"No more than a hundred years, probably less, yes," Nate replied.

"How is that possible?" Curt asked. "Something like that seems really drastic."

"It is. But there are things that could happen. This was a major geological event," Nate answered. "Massive fault activity ..." He pointed to the sky. "That blue moon. It could have moved in orbit causing a drastic change in tides."

"Fault activity," Curt said. "Like this fault you said we're on, the same one we're going to drive on?"

"Yes. I'm not promising we won't have seismic activity along the way. We may," Nate said.

"How far along this thrust fault are we traveling?" Finch asked.

"I think we should go about two hundred miles south then head west," Nate replied. "Looking at my photos, I believe if we go further inland that's where we'll find signs of a previous civilization, if there was one."

"Because of the change in oceans?" Finch asked. "Got that."

"Three hundred miles?" Curt asked. "You realize the rover, top speed, fully loaded only goes forty miles an hour.

Power dies out after six hours. Adding time to recharge, we're talking at least two days there and two days back." He looked at Sandra. "Ben can't make that journey. Are you okay with staying here that long?"

"Do I have a choice?" she asked.

"Go," Ben told her, "I'll be fine by myself."

Curt laughed. "I don't think so."

"I'll stay," Rey said. "Honestly, if you want, I'll stay and watch Ben."

"You're our historian," Finch said.

"Anyone can don a cap with a camera and press record," Rey replied. "I can stay back with Ben. And I can start the ship should you guys not return in the five-day window of no communication."

Sandra shook her head. "No. As much as I want to go with them to explore, Ben could have complications."

"I'm fine," Ben said.

"Will you stop?" Sandra snapped. "You aren't fine."

"Considering yesterday you had me for dead," Ben said, "I'm doing fine."

"As much as I do believe Ben will be fine," Finch said, "Sandra has to stay. That's her job. We will also stay in radio communication for as long as we can. Dr. Gale ..." He turned to Nate. "Chart our course. The rest of you pack a sack. We leave in twenty minutes."

Rey hadn't a clue what all to bring. She didn't foresee having to change her clothes too much, and the food supply was completely a separate thing. Something Colonel Finch was handling. So, she packed simply. A change of shirt, an extra pair of pants, that survival pack she had yet to open and her camera.

While she was excited about venturing out into the new world, a part of her just wanted to stay back.

The thought of riding along in the buggy made her dread even more about being a dead weight. What would she have to contribute? It was the same old, same old with her, and she was starting to get irritated with herself.

She carried her stuff to the buggy and Curt took the bag for her. When he placed it in the back she saw the bottle in there. Rey probably wouldn't have thought anything of it had he not told her about his problems. She flashed a smile and stepped back, looking around. Nate was standing by the rod he set up as a sun dial for telling time talking to Sandra.

"Thoughts?" Finch's voice came from behind her.

Rey jumped a bit. "Sorry." She smiled. "You scared me."

"I'm sorry."

"That's okay. What were you asking?"

"You were deep in thought."

"Not really," she said. "Just looking around. Nervous about venturing out. Self-fighting with myself because I can't figure out why I am on this mission."

"Feeling useless?" he asked.

"Yes, I am."

"You weren't … you weren't talking to Curt, were you?"

"No. Why? Did he call me useless?"

"He made … never mind."

Rey grunted. "See."

"Not see. I'm sure Ben would totally argue your self-diagnosis of being useless. In fact, if you sit on your ass the rest of the mission, that one act of valor was enough for me."

"Thank you."

"Aside from that and being our camera woman, you're the face of the people. All of us are looking at this scientifically. You are here to look at this from a colonist perspective. Would you, could you live here?"

"Sounds a little Dr. Seuss. Would you, could you live right here?"

"Would you, could you eat a pear?"

Rey stared at him.

"Sorry that was the best I could come up with. You're the creative one. That essay …" He whistled.

"Yeah, about that. I really didn't—"

"Shh." He held up his hand. "Quit selling yourself short." His eyes drifted beyond her. "Looks like we're ready to go."

Rey looked over his shoulder, Nate and Curt were getting into the Buggy.

"Damn it," he said. "I wanted shotgun."

Rey smiled. "He says he needs more than four days. Do you … do you think he can get all he needs in the little time here?"

"Who, Nate?"

Rey nodded.

"He doesn't need any more time. I think he has his

answer," Finch said. "Okay, so he doesn't have percentages of this mineral or that, but does he really need more time?"

"I would think so."

"Not really. I mean, the whole purpose of this mission is to see if this planet is suitable to live on, to colonize. Well, we're here, right? We're alive. I think we found our second Earth. And I don't know about you," he said, "I for one cannot wait to get home and tell everyone. At least there's some hope."

EIGHTEEN

Nate never really had problems with people. However, he was exceptionally irritated as he rode in the back seat of the buggy with Rey.

First, he was seated in the front, then he was booted to the back by Curt who was booted from the driver's seat. To top that all off, they paid no attention to anything he said.

"You just went the wrong way."

He'd rub his temple, while staring at his tablet.

They ignored him.

"She's handling well," Finch said to Curt. "Nice job."

"Considering the last time I built the buggy the wheel fell off," Curt replied.

"Eh, these things pop together like Lego."

Both Finch and Curt laughed.

Mouthing a *ha, ha, ha*, Nate shook his head and he heard a small snicker come from Rey. He looked at her. "What?"

"You're funny."

"No, I'm not. I'm pissed."

"I know."

"See." He leaned over with the tablet. "This blue dot is

where I marked where I think we landed. We're supposed to be going down this route, the undeveloped path."

"How do you know we're still not on it?" Rey asked.

"Because we're headed more west. We need to stay south."

"How do you know we're not? A different planet? I mean, Earth's magnetic field is what tells us north and south."

"This has a magnetic field here."

"Yeah, but how do you know we're not going south?"

"One … we veered off. Two, because the needle on my compass points north and we're going west," he said.

"How do you know north is north?'

He huffed out and scooted over.

"I'm just saying …"

"Please don't," Nate asked, then leaned toward the front seats. "Gentlemen, why are we not going on the path I suggested?"

"You said we need to go south west," Finch replied. "That's what we're doing."

"I planned a route," Nate told them. "You knew that."

Finch nodded. "Yes, I did. We followed it for a while."

"Not enough."

"Nate," Curt said. "You had us on a thrust fault. I looked at the imaging, I found another that was going west. What's the issue?"

"The issue is I laid out the route. I was basing it on geographical regions."

143

"Are we looking for something specific?" Finch asked. "I thought this was just exploring?"

"We are," Nate said. "But there were places on the imaging from the satellite that could have been civilizations. Plus, areas I believe are water regions. Areas that could be conducive for stopping for the night. This isn't a vacation and there are reasons I am here. This right here, this expedition, is one of them."

"What do you want us to do?" Curt asked.

"Stop the buggy and turn around," Nate said. "We haven't gone that far. Stop before we get too far off the beaten path and get lost."

"Map the route. We're not stopping."

"Stop the buggy."

"Maybe we should stop," Finch said.

"No, don't stop," Curt said.

"Stop the …" Nate paused when the buggy shook.

"Shit," Curt said. "The wheel."

"Guys," Rey called out.

"I don't think it's the wheel or the buggy," Finch said. Holding onto the wheel caused his entire body to shake.

"It's not the buggy," Nate said. "It's an earthquake."

"Guys!" Rey screamed.

Nate looked at her, then saw she was turned in her seat. When he looked behind him he could see why she shouted.

The entire dirt-based area, which was nature's own roadway, split. Like a wide-open mouth with no foreseeable bottom, the dirt dropped into the hole, and the entire pathway melted away before their eyes.

"Get off the fault," Nate told Finch.

Finch raised his eyes to the mirror. "Oh, shit."

"Pull off."

The ground shook violently, bouncing the buggy up and down and almost out of control. Finch jerked the wheel to the right and off the path. The earth was uneven and the buggy sailed over rocks, landing on two wheels before it slammed hard to the ground.

Nate bounced forward then back from the sudden stop, then jumped from the buggy. His balance was off and he extended his arms to try to stay upright. Walking was too difficult and he made his way back to the buggy, holding onto it for support as he watched the fault vanish as it passed them until it finally stopped a hundred feet away.

"Everyone okay?" Finch asked.

They all responded they were.

"There are reasons," Nate said, "we stay the course. This entire area could be unstable, as soon as the Omni is powered enough to move, we have to move inland."

"Fucking planet," Curt blasted. "Seriously. We aren't here even twenty-four hours; it tried to drown us, then bury us. It's almost as if it has a mind of its own and it's tossing everything at us."

"Tell me about it." Finch scratched his head. "Makes you wonder what the hell else can happen."

Ben tried to laugh but grabbed his chest and stopped.

"Easy there," Sandra said, adjusting his covers.

"I'm sorry, that was funny."

"Yeah, laugh at my mistakes. You're still not out of the woods." She checked his IV. "Do you want to rest back now? It's getting late."

"No, I'm good. It feels better to sleep sitting up," he said. "You know. If you want, we can sleep inside." He nodded at the cot set up next to his.

"You can't sleep in there," Sandra told him. "The pods are too small. And this is fine."

"You don't want to set up your own tent?"

"No. And it's easy to walk out the back of the tent and go inside if I need anything. I'm good in the medical tent. But I'm gonna let you rest. You need to rest. Tomorrow I want to try to get some circulation in your legs."

"Planning lots of activities until they get back I see."

"Oh, sure, wait until I have you try more solid food. We have a couple days to kill. Now rest." She stepped back. "I'm going to start a fire."

"Sandra."

She paused in walking out.

"Thanks for hanging back. I know you wanted to see this place."

"I do, and I will." She shut off the bright lighting unit, leaving only a dim light on.

It was chilly again, not as bad as the night before, and taking a page from Rey, Sandra opted for the feel of being home by lighting a fire.

She wanted a hot dog and wished that was one of the

things Curt had stashed in the jibs. Hot dogs were a staple when she and her sister would go camping. On Earth, the fire wasn't just for food and heat, it was a sense of lighting, but on Noah, the sky was never dark, not really. The blue moon cast a sort of 'one shade' darker twilight feel.

Poking at the fire, Sandra watched the flames and her mind raced with thoughts. She tried to find one to grasp onto, something she could focus on and slip into a daydream. She thought of her sister with fondness and longing. Ben was so lucky to be alive, how she wished she was envious of the others, but she wasn't. What was out in the new world was unknown. She'd have her chance once they returned and safely scouted the area. Although, she had quickly learned the planet wasn't predictable. There was no giant wave on the second day, but she could hear the waves and ocean constantly.

That ... was a monster.

If they colonized the planet she couldn't see people ever enjoying the ocean again.

She wasn't out there long, but long enough to know that Ben was probably sleeping. Sandra wasn't tired. Maybe she'd go in the ship and do some reading. Even though the fire was built away from the trees, she needed to snuff it.

She stood, readied her foot to start kicking dirt into the flames and stopped.

Something was different, it felt different.

What was it?

The fire stopped flickering and for a brief second it didn't move. The temperature dropped and then with a change in the wind, the fire moved in one direction. But it wasn't being blown, it was being pulled. Sandra couldn't feel a breeze at all. The air was dead.

In fact, Sandra couldn't hear the ocean at all. From the relaxing sound of rolling waves to silence, then a steady high pitch, whistling wind.

A sound that was constant.

The fire snuffed out.

She could hear the wind but couldn't feel it. Suddenly she heard a crackling of branches.

Snap-snap-snap-snap.

While she didn't need the light of the lantern, she lifted it and pulled out her pistol. Ben was vulnerable, an animal could be deadly to him.

Cautiously she walked toward the sound that came from deep within the woods. She wasn't going to venture too far in. She didn't need to.

About twenty feet into the wooded area, the brightness of the blue moon dimmed a bit, as if the sky suddenly grew overcast. Believing it was a storm rolling in, Sandra peered up to the sky. She saw what looked like a white cloud covering. As her eyes shifted downward she spotted it rolling in the distance through the trees. The white mist was illuminated by the moons. It looked as if it extended from the ground to the tree tops, thick and swirling, moving in a menacing slow way.

What she first thought was a bizarre fog was something different. It was more than a fog. It didn't pass through the trees, it hit them with such a cold blast, that the branches stopped instantly.

Blurting out, "Shit" and facing the reality that whatever it was, was rolling her way, she spun on her heels, dropped the lantern, and raced back to the Omni.

Sandra didn't waste any time. She ran into the med tent, kicked off the breaks on the cot, and tossed the IV onto Ben's body.

He grunted in pain, waking up. "What's going on?"

Sandra didn't answer. She grabbed the end of the cot, spun it around and without stopping, charged through the rear of the tent and straight up the ramp into the back of the Omni.

Once she had the cot inside, she released it and ran to the ramp.

She slammed her hand into the 'close' lever. "Come on, come on, come on," she beckoned the slow closing ramp.

"What is it? What's happening?" Ben asked.

"Some sort of freak ice front. It's freezing everything in its path and we're in its way." Confident the ramp was closing, she rushed by him toward the front of the ship.

"Oh my God. You have to retract the solar panels," Ben told her, as he slid from the cot holding his side.

"I know. Stay put."

"You need me there?"

"I don't know if we have time." Sandra raced into the pilot's seat. Her eyes shifted about, trying to find the right controls.

"Start the engines," Ben instructed. "You can't retract the panels without them or without going outside to do it manually."

Her hand moved from the solar panel controls to the engines and she began flipping switches. "Please let us have enough power."

"We do." Ben arrived on the flight deck.

"Ben, what are you doing?"

"Helping," he said with a struggling voice and sat down, wincing in pain. "Retract the panels."

"Retracting."

"We have to initiate the secondary thermal protection system and the micrometeoroid shields."

"Shouldn't we be fine with the internal TPS?"

"Doesn't hurt to be sure."

"Where are the …?" Her eyes widened when the windows began to ice over. "Oh God, the windows."

"Initiate." Ben stumbled over and maneuvered the controls. In seconds the window shields came down. He leaned against the chair holding onto his side.

Sandra sat back.

"Interior temp is dropping fast," Ben said. "Sixty, fifty …"

"It's not working.

"Forty-two. Holding steady at forty-two and … no, dropping again. Slower though."

She saw the reading as it neared freezing and Sandra lifted her eyes to the ceiling as the Omni vibrated and series of small *snappings* rang out. She rubbed her arms from the cold. "The ship isn't going to make it, is it?"

"She'll hold." Ben sat in the chair next to her. "I hope."

NINETEEN

Finch called it, "Sort of odd." While Curt claimed calling it the thrust fault was, "Borderline obscene." They bickered some over why it was important to even worry about it, when Rey brought up a point.

"Why is it dumb or odd?" she asked. "Would you want future generations to call it 'Thrust Fault Path'? Plus isn't it our jobs as the Adam and Eves to name things?"

"Only if the original inhabitants hadn't already," Nate said.

"Yeah, buddy," Curt said. "And we're just gonna be able to read their language."

Nate grumbled a bit over the comment. Finch essentially ended the entire argument by saying for conversation's sake, they call that southward fault 'Mount Ararat Road.' Noah's Ark supposedly landed in the mountains of Ararat and they landed on the fault.

Settled.

They were fortunate enough to have made it back to Mount Ararat Road after their deviation. Nate knew they all labeled him immature, but he was serious. They should have never veered off and those apologies he insisted on were warranted. Especially because of Nate's keen sense and knowledge of topography, they were able to find suitable shelter for the night, located a few miles from where they would go west.

Nate suspected all along that was where they'd camp for the night.

He had previously scouted a place to stop. The geography of the area appeared different to Nate than when he viewed it and enlarged pictures. It was unlike anything he'd seen on Earth. He had to rely on his Earth knowledge and the studying of other planets in order to make an educated guess. The pixilation upon enlarging inhibited a perfect view, but it was close to being clear. It appeared to be a small rocky area, covered with minimal trees and a strange foliage. An area a quarter mile inland from Mount Ararat. They parked the buggy off the path with forty minutes of power remaining, ejected the solar cells and covered the rest of the vehicle, to protect it from any elements.

It was a good thing, too.

It started to rain.

It could have been considered a cavern, but Nate likened it to a sea cave, because he believed at one time that's exactly what it was. He expected when he took soil samples to get evidence of such.

The half-moon opening led to a short slope which widened at the bottom.

Nate took a break from his work and stood against the opening, radio in his hand while his arms were crossed. He kept pressing the radio, checking for a signal or a voice.

"Any luck?" Rey approached him.

"No, I didn't think we would. Not here," Nate said. "Doesn't hurt to try. But if Finch can't get through with the one he has, this ... walkie talkie won't work."

"Do you think they're okay?"

"Yeah. It's just a lack of signal."

"So ... tell me again why we ejected the solar panels in the middle of the night?"

"The sun on this planet beats down early," Nate replied. "We have enough power to drive and charge."

"Isn't that counterproductive?"

"No, not really."

"How's it feel to be right?" she asked.

"About all this?" He winked. "Pretty good."

"It's a great stopping place."

Curt approached and gave a gentle congratulatory tap to Nate's back. "Yeah, it is. Way to go. Seriously, thank you. We could be out in this." He motioned his hand outward toward the rain. "We're still on a portion you think was underwater, right?"

"I do." Nate nodded. "That's what I'm testing the soil for."

"How does something like that happen?" Rey asked. "You said it happened fast, too."

"Hopefully, we'll figure it out. I mean, if we find traces of civilization, they had to see it coming. Maybe that holds the answer," Nate replied.

"Why don't we discuss this over dinner," Curt said. "It's done. I have some questions."

Finch could see the three of them walking from the entrance of the cave. Like some sort of papa bear, he had set up the short folding stools for the meal. The cave seemed to scream for the ambiance of a fire, but he wasn't certain of the ventilation and so he settled for what was called the bright box. A square unit that luminated on all four sides and heated on top.

He warmed a stew for everyone and the premade coffee. Those two things along with crackers and astronaut brownies were a good enough meal.

"Anyone need water?" Finch asked.

"Think we have enough outside," Curt replied. "Did you get any?" he asked of Nate.

"To sample? Yes," Nate replied.

"Good, because that rain along with the ocean from hell seems to be the only water we've seen," Curt said.

"I believe, if we stay the course, we'll find water tomorrow. It looks like it on the imagery."

Rey sat on the little stool, her plate balancing on her knees. She lifted her coffee cup. "Where there's water, there's life."

"Can you imagine the life, if there is any, in that ocean?" Curt asked. "I imagine something massive, prehistoric and monstrous."

Nate nodded. "Yeah, my childhood obsession with Godzilla surfaced a little yesterday."

"Whatever happened on this planet must have been some major event," Curt said.

"I concur," Nate replied. "Enough to cause a massive extinction."

"That we know of," added Rey. "I mean there's not been

a single extinction event on Earth that wiped out a hundred percent of life."

"So where is the life?" Curt asked. "I haven't seen anything alive here. No animals, I would think something would appear."

"I have a theory on that," Finch said. "Animals have an amazing sense of survival. They aren't here because this is a dangerous area. They know it. We happened to land in a bad spot."

"Ya think?" Curt joked.

Finch smiled. "Plus, we don't know what is further inland and we may never know. This is a big area and we are time limited. Imagine if visitors from another planet landed in northern Canada or even Alaska. They could wander around for days and never see a soul."

"They would see lights from space," Nate said. "But then again, if there is intelligent life here, they may not have lights."

"I know it's only been two days," Curt said. "Have you determined anything about this place?"

"It's not a twenty-four-hour day," Nate replied. "More like twenty-three. We've traveled, what, two hundred miles south and already the weather is different, warmer. While the planet is stable, it's certainly proving to be unpredictable. It would take months and years to be able to figure it out to some degree. I'm actually really envious of our terraformers and colonists that will come here in fifty years."

"Why is that?" Finch asked.

"I mean, think about it. We may be like Christopher Columbus, but we will not get to make this planet home. Learn it, love it, name everything from mountains to rivers, towns and cities. Just ..." Nate scraped his fork through his food. "To be honest, if they would let me I would stay. I'd take the jibs and do what I could, get things started. Those who arrive later would have that information. I'd do another time capsule." He softly chuckled. "I'm good at those."

"Why?" Rey asked. "Why would you want to stay here ... alone?"

Nate forced a sad smile. "Because I have absolutely nothing left for me at home."

Finch felt for him, he really did. He knew Nate only from working with him, but he knew enough to know Nate just stopped living outside of work when he lost his family. While others on the crew had little to no family, they had lives outside of work ... friends.

Nate never mentioned a single friend. He wrapped himself in The Noah Project.

Finch cleared his throat. "I say this sincerely, Earth needs you. You are one of the greatest minds in this field. If not the greatest. However, your focus is saving the future of mankind. You could do that here. Ensure man's survival. If when we leave, you truly believe you want to finish your work here ... I'll respect that, the jibs have everything to start here. You wanna stay, you can stay."

"What?" Curt blasted. "Are you nuts? You can't leave a man behind!"

"I think that choice should be left to anyone on the team," Finch said. "I don't want to leave him behind. But isn't our job, isn't this mission to find out if this world will work for future generations? As long as we bring back the answer, what does it matter if he's Robinson Crusoe?"

"You're insane," Curt said.

"Probably." Finch smiled. He couldn't believe he'd actually made that suggestion to Nate, it came out of his mouth before he even gave it a thought. But in hindsight he didn't regret it.

The conversation stayed serious only briefly then it lifted in mood. Joking around about who would stay behind, and Curt claiming he didn't bring enough booze for that.

Eventually, it calmed and everyone settled for the night. Nate continued working. As captain, Finch didn't feel comfortable with him moving about the cave. He couldn't fall asleep until he knew Nate was safe. He waited, listening for him, while reading by the light of the bright box. As the hours rolled by and the pages kept turning on his book, Finch grew tired.

He decided to check on Nate and request he rejoin camp for the night.

He grabbed the lantern, stepped over a sleeping Curt and followed the dim light that came from a branch of the cave.

Walking toward the light, Finch heard a scarping sound. It stopped and he heard whispering.

"Nate?" he called out softly.

"Yeah?" came his muffled answer.

Finch walked closer. Nate was on the ground, a tiny pick and lantern by him and a pen light in his mouth. "Who are you talking to?"

He took the pen from his mouth. "Myself. Sorry."

It was then, Finch noticed Nate's fingers were rolled to his palm as if holding an item. "Did you find something?"

"Actually, I did." He lifted it. It was circular and about two inches in diameter. "I don't know what it is. It's pretty encased in rock. I can't really ... see. It's coming up metal, see." Nate lifted a phone size instrument and held it over the object. The instrument beeped. "That's how I found it."

"Metal? For real?"

"Yeah. I mean, it could be nothing." He extended it to Finch.

Finch took it in his hand. It really did feel like a rock upon first touch. Rough and thick all over, until he rolled it between his forefinger and thumb. "I see what you mean. It feels metal. It has an edge."

"We have to be careful. We don't know how old it is. I'll get a better look in the daylight, but when we get back to the Omni, I can clean it and clear it without damage."

"I'm excited." He handed it back.

"You sound it. What made you look for me?"

"Oh, it's late. Do you feel like wrapping it up for the night? I would just feel much better if we were all together when I went to sleep."

"Um ... yeah. I suppose I can always come back here. Bring better tools."

"I'd appreciate it," Finch said. "See you back up there."

"Finch."

Finch stopped.

"Did you really mean what you said? You'd allow me to stay behind if I wanted to?"

"Yeah." Finch nodded. "I did."

"Thank you for that."

"You're welcome for that. Now ..." Finch waved his finger. "Finish up. Please."

"I'm right behind you."

"Good night." Finch began his return but paused a few feet away to look back to make sure Nate was gathering his items. The determined geologist was examining his find. Holding the round object in his hand and close to the light.

It didn't surprise Finch at all that Nate found something. In fact, he expected it. If anyone would, it certainly would be Nate. And Finch was also sure it wasn't going to be the last discovery made by Dr. Nathan Gale.

TWENTY

"Okay, you need to stop," Ben told Sandra as she tried the rear hatch once again, banging her shoulder against it over and over. "You're wasting energy and oxygen."

"We wouldn't need to worry about oxygen if you let me start the ship again." She pulled the mylar blanket over her shoulders.

"We're not starting the ship again. There's no need. We have to build the power supply. Not use it. Give the sun time to do what a sun does best. Okay?"

"We need to get out."

"Yeah, we do."

"We're stuck in here."

"No, we aren't," Ben said. "Yes, it's cold. I know. But the solar panels ejected without a problem. That tells me we aren't stuck."

"That we can see," Sandra argued. "Which we cannot. The shield and doors are frozen."

"Give it time. I know this ship well. We're fine. I promise you if in two hours the hatch or ramp doesn't open we can fire up the ship again."

"Any contact with the team on the radio?"

160

"No. I don't expect to. If they're hundreds of miles away, we won't get a signal. Especially if the antenna is frozen. We'll know when it defrosts."

"What do we do in the meantime?"

"You can sleep. You haven't slept. Sit down. Close your eyes and get some sleep. Now, Captain. I outrank you so that's an order. Sleep."

Disgruntled, Sandra plopped down into the pilot's seat. She was tired, really tired, but she wasn't sure if she could sleep at all.

She did.

Before she knew it, she was out and when she jolted awake, she believed that only a few minutes had passed. She was wrong.

The main door to the omni was open wide and the ship had warmed up. She stood from the seat and looked around, tucking her long bangs that fell from her messy bun behind her ears.

"Ben?" she called out. "Ben?"

When she saw him limping and walking slowly to her, holding tools, she got annoyed. "What are you doing?"

"My job," he said. "My job is the mechanic. I'm making sure everything is alright."

"Is it?"

"Yeah. Yeah. Nothing I can see. As far as I can tell we made it through whatever that event was. I don't want to fire her up because we'll have enough power when they get back to fly off, use her as a plane."

"To go home," Sandra said. "We need to go home."

"No, we don't. Not yet. I'm alright. Not a hundred percent. In pain. Trust me, I'm in pain. Plan on stealing Clutch's stash, but I'm alright. I don't want to leave. Do you?"

Sandra folded her arms close to her body. "No. Not really. I want to see what this place holds beyond natural disasters that pop up out of the blue."

"Me too." Ben smiled. "I do need to sit down right now, though."

Sandra took the tool kit as he hobbled to the step on the door to the Omni and sat. She stepped forward finally looking around at the area after the frost storm.

The sun was so bright in the sky, it was perfectly blue and the bigger moon could even be seen. It almost looked fake, translucent.

The lush green area that had surrounded them went from looking like summer to the dead of winter, even with the warm temperatures. There were no leaves on the trees, they lay all over the ground and the branches dripped water as they defrosted.

Ben had told her the ship was fine, it made it through the phenomenon. Sandra was happy about that, but she worried they had lucked out once, could they survive another night like that? However, the way the planet behaved, the next thing would be fire from the sky. She shuddered at that thought, put it out of her mind, and continued to explore the ravaged area.

◇◇◇◇

It was the rushing sound of water that caught Finch's

attention and caused him to bring the buggy to a stop.

"What's going on?" Nate asked.

"Check your imagery," Finch said. "There's water near here."

"There's water where I want to stop." Nate opened the image. "It's not supposed to be for another thirty miles by my estimate."

"Your estimate might be off. I hear it," Finch said, turning off the buggy. "It's through there." He pointed toward the trees. "It has to be close. Listen how loud it is."

"I don't know about that," Rey said. "We heard the ocean miles away."

Curt pointed. "If that sound is miles away, I'd have to wonder what it could be."

"One way to find out." Finch stepped from the driver's seat and walked around to the back. He lifted the hatch while the others got out and he grabbed his backpack.

Curt reached for his, as did Nate.

"Ready?" Finch asked. He looked over at Nate who was working on his tablet. "What are you doing?"

"It's obviously water. I'm marking it as such."

Finch led the group into the woods and noticed Rey was lagging behind. "Rey? Everything okay?"

She peered up to the sky then looked at him with a smile. "I just saw something flying in the sky." Her voice then upped with enthusiasm and she spoke quickly. "I just saw something in the sky. I saw it."

Nate raced back to the path to look, he kept staring at the sky. "I don't see it."

"It was there," Rey said.

"Water. Life," Curt added. "Bet where we find that water, we find more life."

They headed back into the wooded area. The sound of water increased, and it wasn't a monstrous thing or far away, the reason it sounded loud was because it was close.

They felt the cool mist of water before they saw it and emerged from the trees to a breathtaking sight.

A large cliff was before them, smooth in the middle with rocky sides that came out like shelves, creating a natural staircase. Down the center flowed a rushing stream of water that emptied into a small but beautiful lagoon.

"Wow," Curt said. "I feel like Charlton Heston in the *Planet of the Apes*. No one skinny dip. The natives may be around."

"This is amazing." Nate lifted his tablet and took a photograph. "Are you getting this, Rey?"

"No." She reached up to her camera cap. "I am now."

"What's next?" Finch asked.

"Explore the area." Nate crouched down by the pool of water and placed a sampling tube in there. "See what's around."

"Looks pretty flat up top," Curt said. "The waterfall isn't wide. I'm thinking that's not a lake up there. Maybe a river or stream."

"We can do a flyover once we get back."

"We could wait for that." Curt placed his hands on his hips. "Or ... we could go up."

"Go up?" Finch asked.

"Yeah." Curt nodded. "Go up. I'll go up there."

"Are you nuts?" Finch barked.

"No. It can't be more than a hundred feet. But imagine what I can see from up there." He set down his pack and opened it. "I can make it up the side rocks and it's not that hard from there. I can do this. Plus ..." He handed a radio to Finch. "These should finally work here. I'll radio from up there."

"You're really serious?" Finch asked.

"I am. And curious."

"Be careful."

"You got it." Curt, with his pack, backed up to walk around the small lake.

"Wait," Rey called out. "I'm gonna go with you. I won't go all the way to the top, but I can have your back on those shelves."

"You sure?" Finch asked her.

"Positive."

"Thanks," Curt told her.

Even though Finch found the idea of them climbing dangerous, he did think it was a good idea. He stood with Nate watching as they made their way around the lake to the side of the cliff. They both made it up the first twenty feet with relative ease.

"I don't know if I can watch this," Nate said. "I think I'll take some soil samples."

"I'll see if I can spot anything in the water."

"Good idea. How are you going to do that?"

"By going in."

"Hold off until I test that water." Nate not only had a backpack, he had a small case. He opened it and pulled out a handheld reader. He retrieved a testing strip, dipped it in his specimen, then inserted it in the reader.

"What are you checking for?"

"Bacteria levels. Chemicals." The device beeped, and Nate looked down. "Shit."

"What?"

"I can't see the display …" He moved it around left and right, then he froze.

"What's wrong now?"

"Oh my God." Nate slowly stood.

"What does it say?'

"It's not what it says, it's what I think I see."

"Feel like clueing me in?" Finch saw Nate unzip his suit. "Hey. Hey, what are you doing?"

"Seeing if it's my imagination." Nate stepped from his suit, then the remainder of his clothes, and hurried toward the water.

"So, when I was twelve …" Curt grunted as he made it to the final tier of the cliff, reached down, and extended his hand to Rey. "My grandmother called me Spidey, you know, like Spider-man, because I climbed everything."

Rey climbed up and joined him on the same level. "Is that so?"

"Yeah, I was pretty good and you're doing well, too."

"I was always good at climbing," Rey replied. "Running not so much."

166

Curt looked up to the ledge that was above his head. "Now this one will be tough."

"I'll wait right here for you."

"Sure you don't want to go up? It's one more?"

"I'm sure."

Curt looked around the ledge for something to grab and brace. He spotted a root to a tree and reached for it. When he did, he looked down. "Well, son of a bitch. I told him not to go skinny dipping. Look out, the natives will come now."

Rey peered down. Curt wasn't joking, sure enough when she looked, Nate, wearing only a pair of boxer shorts, had jumped into the lake.

Finch felt like he was watching some long-distance tennis match. His eyes went from Curt slowly taking that final section of the cliff to Nate swimming the short distance across the lake to the waterfall.

All while he stood on the beach trying to determine who he should focus on more.

He brought the radio to his mouth. "Curt, I know you're climbing. Radio me when you're up top. Over." He placed down the radio and looked across the lake when he heard a loud squeal of delight.

Nate was touching the wall near the falling water and he looked back at Finch.

Was he saying something?

Finch lifted his hands, palms outward trying to convey that he was curious about what Nate was doing.

Mixed with the rushing water, Nate said something.

"I can't hear you!" Finch shouted. "What?" He cupped his hand to his ear.

Nate yelled something again, then returned to the wall of the cliff.

"Swell," Finch said. He looked at Curt again, he was almost at the top, then back out to Nate.

Nate emerged from the waterfall and shouted.

Didn't he get that there was no way he could hear him? Finch again lifted his hand, only this time to show him he hadn't a clue what he was saying.

Nate must have understood because he began swimming back.

Seeing him return, Finch reached down to grab Nate's clothes. When he lifted them the circular object Nate had found the night before dropped to the ground.

Finch released the clothes and grabbed the object. He examined it and then rubbed it with his thumb. Then he took what small bit of thumbnail he had and scraped against the rough service. He did so hard and a small piece lifted off.

When that happened, Finch saw that it was indeed metal. Tarnished, but metal. He stared at the cleared small section, trying to see what it was. Then he noticed Nate was close, and Finch placed the object in his pocket.

Despite turning her head, dirt fell down on her face when Rey looked up, watching Curt climb. His slipping boats sent the loose earth her way as she hoped and prayed in her mind that he'd get over the top and do so safely.

She worried.

But she knew once he made it over the ledge, he had the rope, he could secure it to something so he could make it down easier.

Finally, he made it to a point where he could hoist his body over.

"Ha!" he yelled down. "I made it."

"How's it look?" Rey shouted. She titled back, only enough to know she couldn't see him anymore. He was over the edge and topside.

"I don't know. I ..."

"Curt!"

Nothing.

"Curt!"

Curt appeared and yelled over the edge, "You have to come up."

"What? I ... I can't."

"Hold on!" he said and then disappeared from sight. A minute later, he yelled, "Watch out," and the rope came down. "Grab it." He stood at the top. "I have you. You have to come up."

Rey looked at the rope.

"Please."

She took hold of the rope, grasping it firmly. She didn't have the upper body strength to climb the rope straight to the top, so she used the side of the cliff for her feet to leverage and walk as her arms pulled and she moved slowly, hand over hand.

Once she was close, Curt extended his hand.

Rey was fearful to take it, she was so far above the

ground.

"I got you. Take it," he said.

Rey hesitated, scared to let go.

"Come on. What is it they call me? The Clutch."

There was a bizarre sense of comfort in hearing that, and braving the moment, she let go with her right hand. As soon as she did, she felt herself losing her balance and grip, but that was short-lived, Curt grabbed her.

He lived up to the sensationalized name the media had given him.

With a firm grip on her wrist, Curt pulled her up and Rey used her feet to help get to the top. Once there, her chest against the crest of the cliff, Curt grabbed her by the ass end of her suit and hoisted her the rest of the way.

She landed sideways on the flat surface.

"Are you okay?" he asked, standing above her.

"Yeah, I'm fine. Thank you. I can't believe I came up here."

"Well, that's not all you're not gonna believe." Again, he extended his hand.

Rey took hold of it and he aided her to stand. When she did, he turned her to look west and Rey nearly lost her breath.

Nate crawled partially on hands and knees the last few feet out of the lake. Dripping wet he rubbed his arms and jumped up and down a little. "Water is freezing," he said.

"I bet." Finch handed him his clothes.

"Thank you." Nate pulled a T-shirt over his head, then

after dropping his wet boxers, stepped into his pants.

"Care to tell me what that was about," Finch said.

"Window." Nate shivered and so did his words.

"Excuse me?"

He stepped into his jumpsuit and zipped it. "I saw a window."

Finch shook his head, confused. "What are you talking about? I'm asking about the waterfall and what you were doing."

"I thought, you know, it was my imagination. Maybe the water was playing tricks on me. That's why I swam out," he said. "Finch, that's not a cliff. That's not a wall of rocks. That …" He pointed. "Is part of a building."

Before Finch could reply, a rush of static rang out from his radio.

"Finch," Curt called.

Finch lifted the radio. "Yeah, what's up?"

"Colonel," he said. "You aren't going to believe this."

"We were never alone," Rey said softly, standing next to Curt. "All those times we wondered if we were alone in the universe. We have the answer."

"Were we that arrogant to believe we were the only intelligent life force?"

Rey shook her head. "This is amazing."

"Yeah, it is."

They both stood in awe and stared westward.

The top of the cliff was vast: a long flat surface, but in

the distance they could see it. A triangular tipped object that merged with a rounder base. The shape was clear, the color wasn't. It was covered in overgrowth and the metal was corroding. Clearly it was a ruin of sorts that either merged with the earth or was in a valley. That much they couldn't determine. They could have easily begun their journey to it to find out what it was, but instead, they opted to wait for the others.

Curt and Rey left the rope secured to a tree at the top of the cliff and climbed down to join Finch and Nate when they radioed that they, too, had information.

"That's a building?" Curt asked, looking at the waterfall.

"That entire thing," Nate replied. "Yes. You can't see it fully. But when you get close there are window frames. It's a building."

Finch ran his fingers down his face. "And you …" He looked at Curt. "You saw a building."

"We think, yes," Curt replied. "It's a good distance away, but it's a building. I think the top of a sky scraper."

"We don't know if it's like the waterfall building," Rey said. "It's fused with the ground. It's hard to tell. It's in the distance."

"What's it like up there?" Finch asked.

"Flat," Curt answered. "At least for a while. The waterfall is fed from a small river that winds north away from the ruins."

"Jesus," Nate gasped out. "You know what this means, right? All of this … this is an advanced alien civilization. Right here. A city. This place can hold answers to what happened here to this world. Whether or not we can make this our home. This is amazing. Beyond amazing."

"We need to explore," Curt suggested.

"Once up top," Rey said. "Really, we can walk there."

"Or," Nate added, "start with the cliff building. I know we can get into that building through one of those windows."

Finch held out his hands, bouncing them slowly up and down in a 'curb your enthusiasm' manner. "I get it. That's the course of action. I think the easiest thing to do is to go up there." He pointed. "And head to that structure they saw. It may not be buried like this building and we could find answers and explore a lot easier than getting into a building encased in rock."

"Then let's do it," Nate enthusiastically suggested.

"Let's … but …" Finch said. "Not yet."

The three of them looked at him in shock.

"Not yet," Finch repeated. "It's not fair. How would you three feel if you were back at camp? This all will still be here in a couple days. You said it's flat up there, right?" he asked Curt.

Curt nodded.

"Enough room to land?" Finch asked.

"Absolutely."

"Good. Then that's the plan. We head home, we get Sandra, Ben, and the ship and we head back here. We came here as a team and it's only right, we get the answers … as a team."

TWENTY-ONE

"Blue," Sandra said.

Ben tilted his head. "Purple."

"Many shades of purple."

"True." Ben laughed. "Oh, and I see yellow."

"For sure the yellow. That's a good sign."

"I'm healing."

"You are. Four days and you are doing better than I expected. By the way, that is the worst bruise I have ever seen in my entire life," Sandra said.

Ben zipped up his suit. "How many men have you seen that flew into a tree?"

"None at all. You are the first one that—"

Static.

"Omni-4 come in," Finch called over the radio.

They had been sitting outside and Sandra stumbled to a stand and raced into the ship to grab the radio. "This is Omni-4. You guys okay? Over."

"We're great," Finch replied. "How's Major Vonn? Over."

"He's doing well."

"We will arrive in camp in approximately two hours,"

Finch said. "Start packing up. Over."

"Sir? Packing up?"

"Packing up," he repeated. "We're leaving. Out."

"What the hell happened here?" Curt asked upon stepping from the buggy when they arrived. He walked to Ben. "You look good. We all thought you were gonna die."

"I'm tough," Ben replied. "And to answer your question, that first night you were gone, some sort of weird frost storm blew through here. Yesterday the wave returned. Fortunately, it stopped the same place it did before, so we were good."

"Weird frost storm?" Finch asked. "What do you mean?"

"Just like it sounds," Ben replied. "Some cold cloud came through, freezing everything. I mean everything, even the ship. I fired her up yesterday and she is working like a charm."

Finch looked at Nate. "What would cause that?"

"We're close to that frozen tundra," Nate replied. "My guess it's making its way south."

"This planet is a hell planet," Ben said. "It's brutal."

"It's better inland," Curt said. "Trust me."

Sandra asked, "Are we going home? Is that what you meant by leaving?"

Finch shook his head. "No. We're going inland, together. We found what we believe is ruins of an advanced civilization. And that's where we're going. To explore that.

175

Hopefully, with what time we have left before we leave we can find out what lived here, how they lived, and more importantly … what the hell wiped them out."

"I'm no geologist," Ben said, "but as far as what wiped out the inhabitants, I'm gonna take a wild guess and say … this planet."

Nate had made markings on the imagery so well that navigating to the area was easy for Finch. Flying there didn't take long, only about twenty minutes. Packing up to go took most of their time. They had to disassemble the buggy and prepare everything else. Excavating equipment, ropes, and other items for their exploration. They knew what they were going into, at least they believed they did.

At the very least, they had the building encased in the cliff. They talked about entering there if the ruins of the city were impossible to reach.

While they wanted to explore more of the planet, exploring the ruins was vital. It would tell them so much. Knowing how those who lived on the planet died, would allow them to know if those from Earth could survive there.

During the preparations to leave and the short flight, they spoke about what they could find and what they hoped to find. They didn't expect the language to be understandable, but a few things were universal. Such as images.

They hoped to find pictures, paintings, anything that could tell a story. Perhaps, if fortunate, a technology far advanced from Earth's they could use.

The single object that Curt and Rey had spotted was the beacon, and the landmark that told them they had arrived.

They could see it as they flew in.

The structure sat close to an edge of what appeared to be another ridge.

Finch could have circled around, instead he opted to land, bringing the Omni within a hundred feet of the odd-shaped structure.

Once landed, they all stared at it through the window of the Omni before leaving the ship. Being that close, they knew it was part of the ground, much like the building behind the waterfall.

They could see the land dropped off behind the structure. Were there more ruins there?

Nate felt like a kid at Christmas. This was not what he saw on the satellite images. What he believed were structures were deep within trees. This city before them was more in the open.

They all stepped from the ship together, and before setting up camp, before grabbing equipment they needed, they walked to the single structured ruin.

Closing in, Nate knew it couldn't be the only one. "There's a drop off behind it. Maybe a cavern. Bet there's more down there."

The group followed behind, with him taking the lead, walking faster than the rest the closer he drew to it.

Weed-like plants and trees grew around it. The round base tilted into the ground. The pointed top was rusted metal with vines and a moss covering it.

"What could it be?" Ben asked.

"Perhaps the top of a building," Curt suggested.

"Maybe it's part of their technology," Sandra said. "It doesn't look like something livable."

"Nate?" Finch asked. "Any guesses?"

Nate didn't answer, he just moved closer. It was large. At least four stories tall. And before they knew it, they were upon it.

"You know what this reminds me of?" Rey asked. "The shape I mean, only bigger. Ever see those corn silos they have on farms."

Nate could hear everyone else agree with her assessment as he inched his way near it. He didn't respond or join their conversation; his focus was on the structure.

"Are you getting footage of this?" Curt asked.

"I am," replied Rey. "Nate, can I get closer?"

Nate approached it. The thing was bigger than he even imagined. He reached his hand out, touching it. "It's cold. It's definitely metal," he said, smoothing his hand over it. It made sense that it was the top of a building. He was excited. They were going to learn how another planet and people had lived. Were they like people from Earth? Different?

Nate had to examine it.

At first his hand moved slowly, then it picked up intensity, rubbing faster, clearing a spot that contained ages of dirt, growth, and rust.

"Is this something we can enter?" Finch asked. "Is it hollow or solid?"

Suddenly, Nate stopped. Softly, and almost gravelly, he

said, "No."

"No, it's not hollow?" Finch asked. "Or no, it's not solid?"

"Oh my God." Nate stepped back. "Oh my God!"

There was an eruption of laughs behind him, as if the crew found some sort of amusement in what they interpreted as Nate's enthusiasm.

"Oh, God." Nate spun around facing them with sheer panic.

The smile fell from Finch's face. "Nate? What is it?"

He moved from it, hands on head, then paced frantically back and forth. "No. No. No."

"Nate!" Finch scolded. "What the hell?"

"Look at this." Nate pointed. "Look. You know what this is? I know what this is. This isn't some alien structure. This isn't some building … this …" He walked back to it and slammed his hand into it. "Is the International Space Station. It fell from the sky. Oh my God." Nate brought his hands back to his head as he dropped to his knees. "We're home."

PART FIVE: THE DISCOVERY

TWENTY-TWO

"No," Curt said strongly, waving out his hand, presenting as if he were in the mood for a fight. "No." He had walked over to the ruins for a closer look. "You're wrong."

"I'm not wrong," Nate said sadly. "Don't you think I want to be wrong. But I'm not on this one."

"I actually don't think you want to be wrong," Curt told him angrily. "You're the one who wanted to stay behind. This shouldn't affect you at all."

"So you think I would lie?"

"Actually, yeah, I do."

"Guys." Rey stepped forward. "Enough. Okay. Look ..." She faced Nate. "Tell me why you think this is the space station? This isn't that big. Where's the rest of it, if it is?"

"Broken up into pieces when it fell. That's my guess. This is one of the modules."

"How can you be so sure?" Rey asked.

"Because of the Russian markings. Take a look." He pivoted to Curt. "Go on, take a look. It's right there. This is the Zvezda Module. It's rusted, but not hollow. We can go in."

"Oh my God," Sandra groaned out. "This isn't

happening. This can't possibly be happening."

"Makes sense, doesn't it?" Ben asked. "I mean, Einstein theorized wormholes were for time travel."

Curt laughed. "You're saying we time traveled."

Ben nodded. "We did if we are back on Earth."

"We are," Nate said.

"We aren't," argued Curt.

"Jesus," Nate snapped. "Then explain this." He pointed at the module.

"Salyut Eight." Curt nodded with assurance. "It's Russian programing, very similar. The modules actually inspired the Zvezda."

Nate scoffed. "There was no Salyut Eight."

"Actually," Ben added. "Salyut Eight is supposed to be the Zvezda."

Curt shook his head. "No. That's seven. Eight was a military project. It didn't get off the ground, or so the Russians said. It doesn't matter because Salyut Five and Six weren't accounted for, they assumed they fell into an ocean. What if, like NOAA, one of those made it through the Androski. It would have been decades ago and would explain how this looks."

"That makes sense," Sandra said brightly. "It really does."

"It makes more sense than this being the space station. Think about it," Curt said. "The space station was in orbit when we left. The global flooding that Nate talked about, he said that took a hundred years, it happened fast ... however ... this planet has one major continent; it took millions of years for Pangea on *our* Earth to form, and hundreds of millions of years more for it to pull apart. If this was Earth and we time traveled, we are either way back in time, which we're not, because there's a building in the waterfall. Or we're millions of years in the future and that building wouldn't have existed."

"Unless, you know," Ben said, "there was another civilization after us. Plus, if we're dealing with time travel, who is to say the space station didn't go through after us and come through before us. It could have happened, and then we would be a million years into the future."

Nate laughed. "There's no way … millions?" he ridiculed. "You're forgetting evolution, Curt, in millions of years the trees and the plants would have evolved … what about the bacteria in the water? Who are you trying to convince here? Us, or yourself?"

"You don't know everything, Nate," Curt snapped.

"I know this. We are on Earth, but we are only centuries, if not less, in the future from when we left."

"You're spouting sci-fi bullshit," Curt spat.

"We went through a damn wormhole!" Nate shouted.

"Enough!" Finch hollered out, then calmed his voice. "Enough." He rubbed his hand harshly across his face. "Curt, I get it. I do. You are in denial. It's hard I—"

"I am not—"

"Let me finish," Finch said. "It's hard to believe, we don't want to believe it. I myself tried looking for a logical explanation. Then denied it. But, Dr. Gale is one hundred percent correct. We are on Earth." He held up his hand again, when Curt tried to talk. "He found something two days ago, I think he forgot. I've been cleaning it. As much as I want to believe this was an alien civilization, I hardly think they would have a British two pound coin dated 1997." He handed it to Curt. "We're home. Now let's find out what happened here."

TWENTY-THREE

There was work to be done before they explored. The buggy had to be reassembled, and an emergency ladder was secured and rolled over the cliff by the waterfall. They also executed the pully system to lift anything that was found from the ground to the Omni.

After that, they began digging in.

Before any further discussion or exploring, Finch wanted a full camp set up. Nate tested the nearby river water and it was safe. It fed the waterfall; the ground surrounding it didn't show any signs of recent flooding.

It was already an emotionally exhausting day, the last thing Finch wanted was the crew to return from checking out ruins and be too tired to create a proper sleeping environment. Rest was essential. Plus, the control freak in him wanted everything in order. So much so, he inspected camp before assigning areas of exploration.

There were three different zone, so they paired off. He gave them instructions to return to camp in two hours.

It wasn't much time.

Especially not for Rey and Sandra who were given the area beyond the module.

There was no fly over, so it was only with a sense that

187

something was out there.

The women asked to be paired up and to have that area, much to the dismay of Finch. But neither woman wanted to get wet looking at the building in the cliff, and they knew nothing about the module. Finch did.

He really didn't want them to go out to the area alone and kept repeating it was for the sake of safety. Sandra found that reasoning insulting.

With the sun beating down on them the two women walked the distance to the crest. They began with their jumpsuits fully zippered, but it didn't take long for them to unzip the suits to the waist, both tying the sleeves around them to keep the suit up. It was hot and the ground in the distance waved in ripples from the heat making the proximity deceiving. It was nowhere as close as it looked.

The ground was nearly barren, even with the flowing river slightly north, the greenery seemed to only spread around the bed of the river and not much further. The camp was exposed to the blazing sun. They had no natural protection. The only chance for shade and trees was below by the waterfall. But they had to camp near the Omni as there was nowhere below the waterfall to land.

Rey took a sip of her water and ran the back of her hand over her forehead.

"Are you alright?" Sandra asked.

"Yeah, the heat is stifling." She took another sip, then chuckled.

"Okay, I know I didn't say anything funny."

"No, I was just thinking."

"I could use a laugh. What's the chuckle about? Or is it

one of those things that I had to be there for?"

"No, you didn't need to be there. You may not find it funny, but ..." Rey said. "I was just thinking. When we found the waterfall, Curt made a joke. He said, 'I feel like Charlton Heston in the *Planet of the Apes*.'"

"No," she talk-sung the word in disbelief. "He didn't."

"He did."

"You suppose maybe he's psychic, or had a deep instinct and didn't know?"

"No." Rey shook her head. "I think he looked at that waterfall and lake, thought of the movie and never even considered the possibility. However, we missed the similarities."

"Can you say foreshadowing."

"I know, right, it was right there and we didn't see it."

"I don't think I would have wanted to believe it if I had thought it."

"Me either," Rey said.

"It's still so hard for me to believe that we traveled through time. Although, it had to have crossed your mind. I mean, you wrote all about the wormhole, the Androski."

"Can I tell you something?"

"Sure."

"My essay ... it was fiction," Rey said.

"Well, of course, it was based on theory and—"

"No, I mean like really fiction. When the school told us to do the essay, I just lacked any and all creativity so I merged two different science fiction novels and made them look like my theory in essay form."

189

Sandra stopped walking. "You plagiarized the essay that got you here?"

"Yeah." Rey grimaced. "I mean, who would have thought, right? Tens of thousands of essays. Why would mine stick out?"

There was a brief pause and then Sandra said, "Oh my God, that's hysterical. Still though, if you think about it, it was your theory in an essay form based on stuff you had read. Fiction or not."

"That's one way to look at it."

"You're here. We're here. Whether it is a good or bad thing for us remains to be seen." Sandra sighed. "You know, when I was a little girl I would look up to the sky and stars and think ... each of those stars was a sun, and out there was a little girl just like me, on a planet just like Earth, staring up to the same sky."

"Did you ever think you'd be up there?"

Sandra nodded. "I did. I always knew it was what I dreamed about, even though I went into medicine. I was so shocked when NASA accepted my application. Then again, I do have perfect qualifications, I had no one."

"It sucks. I'm sorry."

"Me too. How about you, did you want to go to space?"

Rey laughed. "Hell no. I didn't even want to go to Canada. I hated traveling."

"You ended up on a hell of a ..." Sandra stopped. They were near the crest. It was no longer an optical illusion of being close, it wasn't more than a hundred feet. "We're here."

Rey lifted her shoulders as she heaved in a deep

190

breath.

They both stood there, pausing before going forward. They had no idea what lay beyond that crest. It could be a huge drop-off and they'd be unable to go down, it could be nothing.

They both started walking again at the same time, picking up the pace the nearer they drew.

"Since learning this was Earth," Sandra said, "I want there to be life beyond this cliff."

"Me too. Nate said life is possible the further we go from the sea."

"Maybe there's a big green valley, with people and a town."

"Children. Life."

"There has to be, right?" Sandra said. "I mean we as mankind cannot be extinct."

They arrived and Rey looked at Sandra. "Or can we?"

It wasn't a drop off, it was a slope, but the top of the crest was high enough to see that at one time there was a city, a bigger one, too.

The green that Sandra wished for was there, only it was growth and trees that surrounded the buildings. Some of the structures were intact, some partially crumbled. It was hard to tell if an event caused their demise or if time was the culprit. Vines and moss grew over everything. But more heartbreaking than the city was the long slope that led to the ruins. Tops of a few buildings emerged from the hillside along with part of a truss bridge, its bracing poking out from the ground like spikes. It was as if the earth rolled in swallowing everything in its path and stopped short of wiping out the city.

Without saying anything, they headed carefully down the slope, they didn't have much time remaining before they had to head back, but they knew, if anything else, they were going to find out what city it had been.

◇◇◇◇

Curt didn't know what to make of him. Finch kept walking away from the module to watch Rey and Sandra ... walk. What was he afraid of? Why was he being so protective?

"They're fine, you know," Curt said, grunting as he struggled to open a hatch on the top side of the module.

"I know."

"Sandra's tough," Curt yelled down.

"I know."

"Rey, not so much."

Finch only looked up at him.

Taking a break, Curt climbed down and walked over. "They made it."

"Yes, well, we don't know what's over that hill."

"Why are you so worried? The planet is barren."

"Is it? We don't know. We're only a couple hundred miles inland and according to Nate, about twenty miles from where the ocean used to be."

"Yeah, how about that?" Curt walked back to the module. "So when were you going to say something?"

"About?"

"About us being on Earth. Clearly, you knew."

"Not much longer than you did," Finch said, joining him. "I started picking at the crust on the coin and it became clear to me this morning when we headed back. I don't know when I was going to say something. I'd hoped it wasn't true."

"I'm still hoping. I mean …" Curt began the climb. "Look at this thing. It's rusted, yes, overgrown … sure. But there is not a single sign of crash damage. No sign of fire, it didn't break up."

"It broke up upon entry."

"But if it landed here," Curt said, arriving at the top portion. "It would be destroyed. It's not."

"I don't think it landed here."

"How the heck do you explain it then?"

"I think something happened. A tsunami or something. Something that caused the ocean to push everything this way. I think it was carried in. I don't know. I'm guessing."

"It does sound logical. Any guesses as to what happened?"

"I think this … right here, what we are seeing is what we were headed toward. This is the aftermath, and the reason we were leaving Earth."

With a clunk and a hiss, the hatch opened. "Yes … ha. I got it," Curt said.

"Good job."

"Wanna check it out?"

"We should."

"I have a question. If we are hundreds, if not a thousand years in the future, then the ARCs left, right? They had to have left and had to of landed here."

"If that is the case then your barren planet comment is moot. There would be people here."

"And if there are people who remained then your worrying is warranted. Unfortunately, unless we run into those people there's no way of knowing what happened here, or when."

"That's not true," Finch said. "We have this, what's below the ridge and the cliff building. The answers are here. We just have to find them."

What was he a child?

Ben felt like it.

"Wear a life jacket," Finch said to Ben and Nate.

"You're kidding me, right?" Ben asked with a laugh.

"No, I'm not. I want you to wear a life jacket. Both of you."

"I'm an excellent swimmer," Ben said. "I won medals in school."

"I don't care. Life jackets."

A life jacket was just another thing to lug around. But not wanting to argue any further with Finch, Ben agreed. That wasn't the last of him being babied.

Ben was certain he could have made it down the ladder, but Finch insisted he be slowly lowered using the pully for specimens. He still had to hold on, and he felt badly for Finch and Curt when they lowered him. He wondered if they thought about how he was going to get back up.

Climbing would be a slow process.

Overall, though, going with Nate was the best option. Even hurt, he wasn't useless in the weightlessness of the water. He swam with ease, and was finally moving without pain. He even carried tools with him as he followed Nate to the waterfall.

The life jackets made it difficult to move quickly, but the jacket did remove some added pressure his body was feeling.

Despite that, Nate kept pointing to the building, though Ben didn't see it. When he did think he caught a glimpse, the rippling water and mist of the waterfall made him dismiss it as an optical illusion.

Until he was there under the fall.

He didn't even need to tread water once he got behind the falling water. There were large stones, or something that made it easier to stand.

Whether or not the building was evident within the entire cliff, the section behind the water was clear as day.

"My God." Ben ran his hand over a portion of a window frame. "This is an office building."

"Or apartment. It's hard to tell."

The windows were four feet high, all of them identical and uniform. Behind the waterfall they were able to clearly see about a thirty-foot wide section of a three-story building. Other parts were buried deep beneath rock, fused with the earth.

While it was clear there were windows and frames, it was unclear whether the glass was actually there. It was possible the inside of the building had been hollowed out from time and filled with dirt, rocks and mud that filled in the gaps, like placing Play Dough in a mold.

"Concrete building or brick," Nate said. "I'd scan it, but I didn't want to bring the instruments in the water."

"You mean scan it to see if it has any hollow openings?"

Nate nodded. "If it does, I want to get inside."

"Yeah, me too. Well … one way to find out." Ben pulled out a pry bar. "Pick a window."

TWENTY-FOUR

There was a stench of old and stale that pelted Curt the second he popped his head into the module. It had been air tight and popped like a vacuum-sealed can. He extended a light inside and looked. Gravity and tumbling had had its effects. If it hadn't been tied down or secured then it collected in one large heap at the bottom of the almost erect module. A heap that came a third of the way up the length.

"Was there anyone in there?" Finch asked.

"Not that I can see. She looks empty. But it's hard to tell." He hooked the light onto the interior wall and stepped in carefully. "Seems odd to be in here and not floating. It's like a tin can."

Finch leaned into the hatch. "How does it look?"

"It looks good. There's a lot of salvageable parts in here that we can take if we need them. This whole thing can be salvaged. I mean ..." He checked out the controls that dangled. "Not sure what we would need. Who knows?"

"How about logs, they should be secured?"

"I'm not seeing one, but more than likely"—Curt pointed down—"it's down there."

"Should we start that pile?"

Curt checked out the time. "We have forty minutes until

the others get back. Might as well."

"Do you think the others are finding anything as good?" Finch asked.

"Nah, I think you and I … we hit the jackpot."

"Whoa. We hit the jackpot," Nate said as soon as he stepped through the window.

"What's going on? What do you see?"

Nate stomped his foot to feel for stability. He had chosen the lower floor, feeling it would be best. "It's solid. Come on in."

Cautiously, Ben climbed through. He paused as soon as he was fully beyond the window. The look on his face all but told Nate he was shocked to see the room.

"Still intact," Nate said. "Sort of."

"It's an apartment. Someone's bedroom."

"That's what it looks like … sort of."

In the room was a bed, dresser, and television stand, all covered with a thick gray dust. Half the walls were warped and green while the exterior facing walls, along with the floor, looked like they belonged to a cave. Rocky and firm with some loose dirt. The furnishings were cemented into it.

Nate walked to the dresser and opened the top drawer. "Empty."

"Try the second one."

Nate did. "Empty as well." He turned to face the bedroom door, it was open. "Let's look around. There has to be something in here that will give us a clue."

"Baltimore," Sandra said, as they sat around the fire. "We didn't find much, there wasn't enough time. It started getting dark and time was up. But we know for sure it's Baltimore. We're in Baltimore."

"The module is a lot of work," Curt added. "Everything that was in it is gathered at the bottom. But it is still viable. We just have to sort through it."

"The building in the cliff," Nate said, "is an apartment building … or was. We made it into one of the apartments, the corridor was solid rock. Most of the apartment was just … it was like the rock molded around it. Anyhow, it was empty and it looked like the person left and took all their belongings."

"An evacuation," Finch said.

"They knew it was coming," added Curt. "Which means, people got out."

"Did they survive this massive event though?" Nate asked. "Did humanity overcome it?"

"So … the cliff building probably doesn't have any answers," Finch said. "The module will take some work. Our best bet is to collectively explore Baltimore."

"Baltimore?" Ben asked. "It doesn't make sense. That was near the ocean. We flew inland a hundred miles, at least."

"Yes, but remember?" Nate asked. "The oceans shifted. Everything shifted; I truly believe there was some sort of massive flood. Something which pushed millions of tons of dirt inland."

"Like a giant mudslide," Finch said.

"Yes. Yes," Nate said with a snap of his finger. "Exactly. That would explain the encased apartment building in the waterfall. Mud just rolled in over everything."

"And that would also explain all the buildings that were partially buried," Rey said. "There's a slope after the crest. There are buildings in the slope. It looked like something rolled over them. The equivalent of a mud snowstorm. The buildings at the bottom of the slope, some are destroyed, but a lot can be checked out."

"So we can find out what caused this," Curt said. "Do we know?" He looked at Nate.

"I think we all do," Nate replied and pointed to the night sky. "That. The number one thing that immediately caused us all to not even consider this was Earth." He indicated to the blue moon. "It wasn't there when we left. Somehow that … that planetary object obviously came close to Earth, was slowed down by the gravitational interaction of the moon, or Earth, and was captured into the Earth's orbit."

Finch lifted his views to the sky. "It's huge. It came really close."

"Yes, it did," Nate said. "And we all know how the moon affects the tides and the oceans, plus the gravity. That extra body, as big as it is, threw everything off. The tides, the oceans, the rotation of the earth. Everything."

"So how did the continents all come together?" Curt asked.

"They didn't," Nate replied. "The continents were definitely drifting when we left. In order for them to all come together in some sort of reverse Pangea, it would, as you suggested, Curt, take millions of years. They didn't come

200

together. The oceans receded and changed, and basically buried the other continents. Not all. Those dots of land mass on the satellite imagery are probably what is left of the other continents."

"This is your theory?" Finch asked.

"It is," Nate replied. "A theory which can't be proven unless we find evidence in Baltimore, or we find people. Which I believe we may if we keep going west."

"The human species is resilient," Curt said. "I believe that."

"I do, too," Nate said.

"So we look to Baltimore," Finch said. "Then we go west."

Ben asked. "Is it possible, that if we do find humans, they have evolved?"

Nate half laughed. "No. Because it hasn't been that long."

"What?" Curt asked with a ridicule laugh. "How can that be? We have to be thousands of years in the future."

"If true, do you think the ruins would look like they do?" Nate asked. "No. Walking into the apartment was like walking into a museum. Everything was preserved. Even at that preservation level with windows sealed, contents inside, they would have broken down if thousands of years had passed. Remember how I said when we landed the ocean had only receded about a hundred years earlier?"

Everyone nodded.

"I didn't base that on a guess," Nate said. "I based that on ecological succession. There are three stages. Primary, secondary, and climax. Like going from an empty field to a full-blown forest. Granted, it does repeat and start again, but again it would be only if a hundred thousand years had passed. If an ecological succession had occurred, multiple times in this area, the ruins wouldn't be as preserved as they are."

"How long?" Finch asked.

"None of these trees have reached full maturation. With that being said, we are under a hundred and fifty years since this event occurred," Nate said. "I am basing that on the fact that I have seen primary and secondary succession only."

Curt lifted his hand. "So whatever happened, finished happening a hundred years ago."

"In most places, yes. With the bizarre weather and earthquakes, I'd say it is still on going and hasn't settled," Nate said.

"So that"—Ben pointed to the blue moon—"caused shit to fall apart a hundred years ago, roughly, from right now? That doesn't mean it was a hundred years ago that we left Earth. Hell, we could have been gone a hundred years before it happened."

"True," Nate said. "We don't know when the massive event occurred."

"But we will," Finch said. "That's our first priority. Tomorrow morning we go into Baltimore, we start searching. We not only try to find out what happened …" He looked to each face around the fire. "We try to find out when."

TWENTY-FIVE

Being on the plateau, wide open and with little coverage from nature, Rey found herself on the verge of a sweat from the morning sun that beat against her tent. She had to be doing something wrong with the tent, there just didn't seem to be any air flow. Ben assured her they each had a climate control device. Hers couldn't be working.

Then again, the previous night, everyone but Finch was hitting the bottle. Slightly drowning the woes of finding a destroyed Earth. Finch didn't frown too much upon it considering the circumstances.

She stumbled from the tent, only the second one awake. She could hear the clink of tools, a crack of a wrench, so she followed the sound to see Finch at the side of the Omni.

"Morning," Finch said when he saw her.

"Morning."

"There's coffee on the fire."

"Thank you. Is there something wrong with the Omni?"

"No. Not at all. I'm just setting up the temporary base."

"What's that?"

"Like the medical tent. It was designed for us to dig in for a week or so while here. It allows us to utilize the water

203

recycle system to shower, use the bathroom without popping a squat."

"That would be nice. Could you have Ben check the climate control in my tent? It was rather warm and stuffy in there."

"Sure," he said. "I can do it when I'm done."

"Thank you. What time are we heading out? It's a long walk."

"We'll head out in an hour. We're taking the buggy though."

"I thought it only seats four. Are two of us staying behind?" Rey asked.

"There's a grab bar, stand and belt system for the back. We'll make Nate and Curt hang on." He winked, almost as if he were joking.

"I'm gonna go grab some coffee." Rey pointed back with her thumb. "Thanks again."

She walked over to the small fire. Finch had a tiny fold-out table with the cups already set out and she grabbed one, pouring herself a cup. As she sipped it, she peered over the rim, watching Finch work diligently on setting up the temporary base.

Was it really temporary?

He was digging in.

Long-term.

That made her sad, and Rey tried not to think too much about it. About her brother and family, the friends she left behind, the children in her classes.

Truth was the reality was starting to set in for Rey. As

she watched Finch she recalled the night before they left, when he promised her he would bring her home. It wasn't the way she planned or imagined, but Finch did indeed keep true to his word.

The Interstate ninety-five sign was pretty much all Nate needed to give him the final piece of the puzzle in guessing their location in Baltimore. Sandra and Rey didn't see it the first time they came down the slope, mainly because the lettering faced the opposite way, and the team made their way down slightly more north.

The first recognizable structure was the lights that set on top of the bleachers in the city's football stadium. Part of the building had crumbled, and the slope stopped just around the third level, going through the stadium until it leveled out.

"Looks like the mud wave came from the south, making its way northwest," Nate said staring at the image on his tablet. "Everything south and southeast of the stadium is gone."

"Buried," Rey corrected. "It's still there."

"How did you determine this was Baltimore?" Finch asked.

"It wasn't the stadium," Rey replied. "It was the street cleaning sign that we saw. It was rusted and dirty, but we saw the name Baltimore."

"Do we know what happened here?" Curl asked. "I mean, half the buildings are destroyed."

"Could it have been a bomb?" Ben questioned.

Nate shook his head. "Seismic activity brought things down initially, then time just took its toll … head toward the larger buildings, that's our best bet. I don't think we'll find many answers in this area."

"What …" Curt peered over Nate's shoulder. "What are you looking at?"

"Oh, I'm pinpointing our location on the recent imagery from the Omni, creating a map. Plus, I have a map of Baltimore. You know what we should do? We are not that far from Washington DC. The fault runs past there. It looks clear, we could make it there and back on one charge of the buggy."

"Not sure I want to see Washington, DC," said Sandra. "That would be too much of a nail in the reality coffin."

"I would like to," Finch said. "And that's a great idea. But if anyone doesn't want to come, they can stay back. The module has useful information and technology that can come in handy."

"What exactly are we looking for?" Ben asked. "We have an idea of what happened."

"We need the when and specifics," Finch replied. "We need to know if they evacuated the entire city. If so, they had forewarning, and there is a chance there are people remaining."

"The when is important," Nate said. "I want us to know how far we have come, if the event is nearly done, or how much more we have to face. A date is important. Find anything with a date."

◇◇◇◇◇

"I watched my children die before my eyes," Ben said with so much frustration as he searched a back area with Rey at a medical center they uncovered on the way into downtown.

They collectively believed if anywhere, the hospital would give them answers. The building for the most part was still intact. The interior was thick with dust and dirt along with mold and moss that grew everywhere.

"I watched them die and there was nothing I could do," Ben continued. "They weren't in my reach, I couldn't suddenly become The Clutch and save them. Then my wife opts out. She just opts out. I wanted to, I really wanted to."

"I understand that."

"Of course you do, I'm sorry."

"No ... no. It's fine. What made you not ... opt out?"

"I don't know. But I ended up hating this planet. I hate this fucking planet. I wanted nothing more than for this to be ..." Almost angry, he tossed a package. "I wanted this to be someplace else. Somewhere other than a place that caused me so much pain. And what happens? I'm not here an hour and the planet tries to kill me."

"Nate wanted to stay behind and not return."

"Really?" Ben asked. "What did Finch say?"

"He said he wanted him to return, but he wasn't stopping him if he wanted to stay behind."

"I get that. I do. But ... hey, what difference does it make now? We're already home."

Finch cleared his throat, which caused them both to turn

207

around.

"How's it going?" Finch asked.

"Nothing," Rey answered. "There's nothing here with dates. Just useless stuff. And I mean useless."

"Yeah, we're finding that is the case, everywhere in here. We're ..." Finch pointed back with his thumb. "We're meeting up in the front lobby. Try to figure out what's next. This is a bust."

"Tell me about it." Ben tossed a package of tubing and after waiting on Rey, they followed Finch out.

"Structurally speaking," Curt explained, "this building sustained minimal damage. Finch and I hit two of the upper floors."

"And nothing," Finch said. "Not a single patient. Not any charts."

"Everything we found is useless," Rey added.

"Just tubing and things that no one would want," Ben said.

"In fact, this place is picked clean," Nate said. "Not just evacuated clean. Clean out, picked clean. Not an aspirin or even a Band-Aid."

"Damn it." Finch shook his head. "I really thought this would be a place to get answers."

"What about a hotel?" Rey suggested. "I can't see all records taken from there."

"We can try one," Finch said. "There are a lot of places out there we can check."

"You know ..." Sandra spoke up. "You guys are wrong.

We did get some answers here."

Finch looked at her. "What do you mean?"

"The emergency room," Sandra replied. "Yes, there were no documents, but all you had to do was look around. There were cots lined in the halls. Single patient triage with four or five beds. Something big happened here before the event. I think it was a heatwave. An excruciating heatwave that put a lot of the population here in the hospital. The sheer number of cooling blankets left is astonishing. It was hot here, really hot. I will even venture to guess the evacuation happened over the heat, and long before the earthquake, if there was even one."

"Still doesn't tell us when," Finch said, leading the group outside. "I want to know what time frame we are at. There has to be something remaining that will tell us." He looked down at his watch. "Alright, let's head outside, take a meal break, then head into the main portion of the city. There has to be something there."

Finch paused with the team by him and looked around.

"Why does it matter?" Ben asked. "I mean let's face it, Earth has turned into hell. It's even worse than before, I can wait to see what it throws at us next."

The whistle sound was short, giving no warning. An arrow sailed fast at the group, and before they registered what had happened, it landed with a thud directly into the area above Ben's right knee.

Ben grunted loudly in pain as he dropped to the ground.

Rey was beside him and without hesitation lowered to the ground to aid him. Immediately and instinctively, Finch grabbed his pistol, as did Curt and Sandra.

The three of them raised their weapons, all taking a tactical stance as they shifted their arms slightly left to right, scanning the area.

"The natives have found us," Curt said. "I'm not seeing them."

"Me either," Finch replied. "Where did it come from?"

"Status on Ben," Sandra called out.

"Status on Ben?" Ben asked with heavy breathing. "Status on Ben is Ben is fucking pissed."

"Bleeding. Not real bad," Rey replied.

"Don't remove the arrow," Sandra dictated.

"Listen up," Finch spoke low. "Ben? Can you make it to your feet?"

"Yeah," Ben replied.

"I'll help him," Nate said.

"Good. Do that," Finch said. "Sandra let me know when he's up."

After a few seconds and a mix of painful groans, Sandra whispered, "He's up."

"Good. On my call, Curt and Nate, grab Ben. Sandra and I will cover. Back into the hospital. Retreat. Ready?"

"Lower your weapons!" a voice shouted out.

"Why would we do that? You hit one of my men," Finch replied, trying to spot the man, but he couldn't. He saw no one.

"Yeah, well, we could have killed him. We didn't."

"We aren't here for a fight. We mean you no harm. Let us get our man help. We have guns, you have arrows ..."

A single shot fired and landed a few inches from Finch's boot.

Finch looked at Curt.

"Okay, what now?" Curt asked.

"Get ready?"

"We'll let you walk," the man shouted. "We want all your stuff. Everything."

Curt whispered, "They want our stuff."

"No shit. They aren't getting it." Finch raised his voice to communicate with the man. "That is not going to happen, sir. If there is something you need that we have, we will help you out. We are not giving up our stuff."

"I believe you will want to."

"Why would we do that?"

Another short whistle, another arrow. It sailed down toward the group and landed in Ben's other leg.

"Ug, God, son of a bitch!" Ben screamed.

"I see him," Curt whispered. "I'm taking him out."

"Put your weapons down!" the man ordered again. "Put them down or we'll take you all out."

Upon his words, from the brushes and rubble stepped men and women, there had to be thirty, all armed with bows and a few had guns.

Finch exhaled and readied to lower his weapons.

"Hold up, Pyle. Hold up!" another man shouted from the distance.

A man who looked to be in his sixties broke through the pack.

"Dad? What are you doing?"

"They're harmless. They're lost." The man walked nearer to the team. "This is the crew of the Omni-4."

TWENTY-SIX

The man named Pyle was probably about twenty-three years old, but he had a face that was hardened and rough like a forty-year-old man. He was a big guy, whose size didn't quite match the voice. He was the son of a man name Quinn, who seemed teetering on shock when he approached Finch.

Excitedly, he introduced himself, then his son Pyle.

Finch wasn't as excited. Calmly, in Finch style, he asked, "Pyle, are you responsible for making the call to take my man down?"

When Pyle nodded his acknowledgement, Finch turned to Quinn. "I mean no disrespect. But since I can't just shoot your kid..." Then he nailed Pyle square in the jaw.

Rey winced truly believing that moment would not finish off well. She expected all hell to break loose. It didn't.

While she wouldn't exactly call it an even exchange of pain, it was close enough.

Quinn said he'd explain everything when they got to their village. He offered another apology and a promise they just got off on the wrong foot.

Finch wasn't buying it. Ben needed medical attention, quickly, and he didn't feel comfortable, especially since Pyle demanded their stuff. Why would he leave it and trust them?

"When our scout spotted the fire in the distance coming from the verboten zone, we figured it was a group that fractioned off from us ten years ago. They've caused us a lot of problems in the past."

"I understand that," Finch said. "But it's still no reason for us to trust you. Thank you, but we're heading back to our camp. We'll meet tomorrow, our man needs medical attention."

"We have doctors," Quinn said. "And something for you."

Curt started laughing. "You have something for us? Like you were expecting us?"

"Not expect ... find," Quinn said. "We expected to find you."

"Who ... who are you?" Finch asked.

"We're the Genesis colonists sent here to prepare the planet," he said. "We left Earth twenty-five years after you did."

Quinn's simple statement was enough to drum up the curiosity of Nate's team. It was enough for Nate, especially. It was his way of finding out what happened to the earth, but the questions were abound; most of all how did those who left Earth twenty-five years after the Omni, get there first?

Technology wasn't as stilted as Nate would have believed.

They had solar-powered vehicles much like the buggy they brought with them. Their village was about fifteen miles west of Baltimore, and they took a dirt road to the settlement.

As they approached they were greeted with bountiful farmlands and orchards.

When they pulled into the village, it wasn't the grass huts or tents Nate imagined, but close. The buildings were constructed some of clay, some stone, others logs. They were neatly organized into a community setting with a few bigger buildings that were businesses.

"How long have you been here?" Nate asked.

"Twenty-six years, four months, and two days," Quinn answered. "Quite a while. I was about your age when we got here."

First order of business was to get Ben medical attention. Sandra insisted on staying with him, even though Quinn assured her he was in good hands. She'd meet up with the rest later.

The townsfolk were curious about the arrival of the strangers, but Quinn asked for privacy, and he brought the team to his home where they sat in his yard around a large oak table.

His wife Dana placed some fresh fruit and rolls on the table and offered them some wine while she prepared a meal.

"Please don't tell me you took the world back to the woman's place is in the kitchen?" Rey asked.

"Hardly," Quinn said. "My wife just loves to cook. And I'm sure you all have other questions."

Curt asked first, "You said you were expecting to find us?"

"Yep." Quinn nodded. "I was fifteen years old when I watched your ship take off. I kept thinking, I'm gonna be an astronaut, because I wanted to be on the first ship out to colonize the new world. I ended up doing not only that but was also the commander of both Genesis One and Two. We brought two ships."

"So you were old enough to remember what happened?" Finch asked. "What did they say about us?"

"Well, of course, you never returned. They lost contact with you when you went through the Androski. When you never returned, and the Androski closed, the theory was always that you made it to the planet and were unable to return. Something you were all prepared for anyhow."

"I'm confused," Nate said. "You left twenty-five years after us. We didn't come back, what made them think it would work for you?"

"What choice did we have?"

"Still twenty-five years after us and you have been here that long?" Nate questioned further.

"Wormholes are a tricky thing. Mostly they were always in the mind of writers and Einstein, no one knew anything. We have a gentleman here, a scholar who educated us on Einstein's theories so we could understand this space-time continuum. See, there's no controls with a wormhole. Where you go is where you go. The NOAA came back decades after she left. Since being here, we determined those images it took aren't exactly right. They're probably from about a hundred years from right now."

"Christ," Nate huffed. "It's confusing."

"Don't try to figure it out. I just knew the second we went through we weren't in another galaxy, we were home."

"How?" Finch asked. "How did you know?"

"For starters, the Xbruxus or Planet X as earlier generations called it, was nowhere near this close to Earth when we left. That's that big beautiful and dangerous planet up there. When we came through it was right smack there."

Finch nodded. "We had the same experience. I came to and saw it."

"So you weren't wearing your life support suits?" Quinn asked. "Wait. You wouldn't be. There was no theory that power could be lost when breaching the wormhole. We wore our suits, lost power for about fifteen seconds, floated through and damn near was caught in its pull. Genesis One ended up crash landing. Thankfully only the one ship was ruined. We knew then we were on Earth and had missed the show."

"The show," Nate said. "I'm going to assume you mean the event that changed our world?"

"Exactly."

"Hold on." Nate pulled forth his pack and reached inside. "I want to write this down."

"There's no need. You're welcome to review the data. We were able to retrieve a lot of it from an observatory in former Virginia. On the edge of the verboten zone. It was one of the few intact."

Curt asked. "Why do you call it that?"

"You would too," Quinn replied. "I didn't want to call it the forbidden zone, because we all made those bad *Planet of the Apes* jokes when we got here."

"So it's not because of some odd reason, or a way to control people?" Rey asked.

"No, it's not. It's to keep them alive," Quinn said. "It's calmed down a lot since we arrived here. But at first it was nature's fury at its best. Tidal waves that crashed in, bizarre snow storms, earthquakes, you name it. It's very dangerous there. I'll show you a map. Pretty much Baltimore is on the edge of that zone. It has a lot to do with the ocean."

"It was the planet, though?" Nate asked. "That was the determination. When?"

Quinn nodded. "When you left, things had been falling apart for a few years. Gradually getting worse, continents drifting faster, volcanic eruptions, well, you know the story. No one knew why. I mean, the sun was thought to be the main culprit, or the moon for that matter. Then about five years after your disappearance it was discovered that the planet was pretty much coming in directly behind our moon. When we left, they estimated it would be about two hundred years or so before it was close. There was a fear that it might strike the moon. It didn't ... obviously. When we got here and saw it, we suspected, but hadn't confirmed at first that it was pulled into the same rotation as the moon."

"That's my theory," Nate said.

"We confirmed that at the observatory. We've been here twenty-five years; we have had a lot of time to explore."

Finch lifted his hand slightly, alerting them he was going to speak. "You weren't on Earth when it fell apart?"

"No." Quinn shook his head. "That doesn't mean we don't know what happened. People survived, the story was passed from generation to generation. Documents kept. You don't see other survivors, we're scattered about.

218

Hundreds of miles apart. What we know ... the planet pushed the moon back, it disrupted our tides and rotation. Natural disasters were worse than we experienced. The United States was the first to absorb the wave. They relied heavily on information from the UK. At one point, this entire area was under water. There were portions of the United States that didn't get touched, however. Colorado, Utah, and Wyoming never went under. Eventually Europe went under, but it wasn't before they were able to save about one percent of their population. They moved the ships and subs south and out of the former Atlantic region, because that portion is hell."

"We've learned," Finch said.

"We've taken the Genesis up many times to explore and take pictures."

"How long?" Curt asked. "How long ago? Has to be hundreds of years, right?"

Quinn pursed his lips. "You would think. Timetable tells us that Xbruxus looped into the final orbit about fifty years after we left. That final event happened ninety-two years ago. Sadly, you have been gone one hundred and sixty-seven years."

Finch, Nate, and Curt all sat back taking in the news.

Rey widened her eyes. "That means the ARCs got off the ground."

"We have yet to be able to confirm that. From what we read, the earth pretty much went into peril within a decade of our launch. If they did, they aren't here yet." Quinn looked up when Dana approached holding a long silver case, two feet wide, ten inches deep. It was dirty and in some parts rusted.

"Heavy," she said.

"Thank you, Dana." Quinn pushed the box to the center of the table. "This belongs to all of you. We were given this when we left, in hopes that we would find you in the new world, the Noah. No one ever gave up hope that you were alive."

Finch ran his hand over the box. "What's in it?"

"I don't know. I never opened it. It's yours."

"Can I ask you something?" Finch questioned. "The one Genesis worked, did you ever think to go back through the Androski? Go back right away and tell them?"

Quinn smiled sadly. "That's impossible. The wormhole, as I said, doesn't have a control, there's no knowing where you'll end up. Look at us, we left after you and got here first. Our scientist estimated it's a million to one shot of even coming close to the same time. A hundred years is a blink of an eye. So, no, we never tried."

Finch placed his hands flat on the case, smoothing them over it in wonder while absorbing the information he had received.

Quinn had answered a lot of questions that Finch had on his mind. He was certain he'd have more as time moved on. The next big question was what was in the case. For that answer, Finch would wait until his entire team was together.

TWENTY-SEVEN

Quinn provided them a ride back to their camp, cautioning them to move farther west. The drive back was a quiet one, with the occasional gripe from Ben who reiterated he was still angry.

Nate found it funny. Not so much Ben's pain, but Curt's ability to push Ben's buttons. He kept telling Ben, "You have to see the humor in this, right? Everything is happening to you. Wait, unless it's Rey who's your bad luck charm."

"Hey, now," she said. "I resent that."

Nate paid close attention to everyone's demeanor. Sandra was less talkative claiming she had to take in all the information that was given to her. It fazed Ben less than it fazed Nate.

Finch was quiet, the case rested on his lap and his hands stayed upon the surface. As if he were protecting the case with his life.

The driver, Westerman, was first generation New Earth and about eighteen years old. He knew a better way around the slope, at least the steep side. There was no way Ben could walk it, and he declined staying in their hospital.

However, Westerman took the offer to stay the night at the Omni. It was too dark and dangerous to drive back alone.

Once they arrived, it was an unspoken agreement the case would be opened.

Finch was silent when he did. Inside was what looked like a tablet in a case, set in a docking port. Curt immediately put the port in the Omni, but after two hours, the tablet wouldn't charge.

It was dead from years of non-use.

Ben didn't let it go, he took the tablet and assured the others he would make it work.

Inside the case was a letter from the president thanking them for their service and wishing them well in their new land. There were mementos and pictures from their lives that had been in their homes. Items they wouldn't have thought to bring for a short trip.

Newspaper clippings, a few new books, and different things that Tom Waite, the gentleman from NASA, believed they would miss.

They sat around the campfire, looking at the items. Westerman sat back, looking like a third wheel.

"I think we all need to talk," Finch said. "When Ben comes back out …"

"I got it," Ben yelled from the Omni. "Guys, come on. It's a video message. I got it."

Without hesitation they all raced inside to the Omni.

It was an occasion which called for a drink, and even Finch indulged, sipping his, standing in the back watching.

Ben was unable to start the tablet, but rigged it to the ship's computer system.

There was sadness mixed with laughter as the

individual messages were played for them.

Nate's message was first; it was his military friends, guys that he had stayed in contact with and ones who helped him through the loss of his family.

"You are so lucky," the one said. "Hope you find a nice alien woman."

They laughed.

The team laughed.

"Seriously though, take care, bud."

When an older man along with a group of nine men squished into the screen, everyone was surprised the message came for Nate.

Curt gave him a friendly shove. "You never mentioned you had friends?"

"That's my softball team. We've been playing since high school. The older guy is my uncle."

They delivered their messages.

Curt's message was from a slew of women.

Rey's brother and his family all spoke of how they missed her and loved her, how proud they were of her and hoped she found happiness.

Sandra shed more tears than most as a woman came on screen. It was her girlfriend. The woman joked at first about Sandra having to be a new 'Eve' in the new world, then delivered a heartfelt message.

They all wanted to watch their messages again, but Rey needed air. She'd have plenty of time to watch them later. With her drink in hand, she stepped outside and saw Finch standing by the fire.

It was then she realized there was no message for Finch.

While everyone else always threw out there they had 'no one left,' that wasn't entirely true. They did: friends, distant family, significant others.

"Hey." Rey approached him.

"Hey. How was …" He cleared his throat. "Getting those messages?"

"It was nice."

He nodded.

"Finch … I'm sorry. I'm sorry you didn't have a message."

He looked at her. "I'm happy for you all. Just … it took the messages for me to realize I was really alone in the world." He cleared his throat. "I'm used to it."

"You said before we went into the Omni we needed to talk."

"Yeah, we do." He looked beyond her to the Omni. "And when everyone comes out, we are going to do just that."

They all sat around the fire, and Finch walked to each person, handing them a small square, blank piece of paper and pen.

"What's this?" Curt asked.

"I said we needed to talk," Finch said. "This is your vote." He held up a square. "We got here. We found out where we are. We haven't talked about what we're going to

224

do. Quinn invited us to live in his village. Set up camp there until we have housing. Integrate ourselves. Or we can find our own place to set up."

"Is that what we're voting on?" Nate asked.

Finch shook his head. "What we do, where we set up, is all contingent on what you vote to do. We came here as a team and we'll make the decision as one. I want you to vote whether we stay, or we take our chances and go back through the Androski."

Ben stared at his square. "I didn't think it was an option. I thought that was your call."

"It's not."

"It's a wormhole," Nate said. "You heard Quinn, chances are we won't go back to our own time."

"We could end up in the middle of everything," Rey said. "Or thousands of years in the past. It's a crap shoot."

"But there's a chance we will, or maybe even might come close. The NOAA did, right?" Finch said. "We need to all agree that whatever the majority decides is what we will do. Agree?"

He watched as they all nodded.

"Wait. Wait." Curt held up his hand. "There are six of us. What if it's a tie?"

Finch bent down and lifted a tin cup. "In here are two slips of paper. One says stay, the other says go home." He walked the cup over to Westerman, who sat by his own tent. He handed it to him.

"What? Me?" Westerman asked.

"You'll reach in and grab the deciding vote," Finch told

him.

Westerman took the cup.

"Okay," Finch returned over to the fire. "Vote."

It was quiet except for the crackling of the fire. There was a sense of nervousness within the group as Finch lifted each sheet of paper, unfolded it and read the anonymous vote.

"Go." Finch pulled the next one. "Go ... stay." He pulled another. "Go." Another. "Stay." He reached inside for the final vote. He opened it, raised his eyes and then read it, "Stay."

"Tie," Curt sighed out. "How did I not see that one coming?"

"Again," Finch said as he stood. "We are all in agreement that we do whatever is pulled from the cup?" When he got their agreement he walked over to Westerman. "Please pull one."

Westerman shook the cup and reached inside. He removed the vote and handed it to Finch.

Finch opened it.

TWENTY-EIGHT

"I'd like to officially announce," Ben said, "there isn't a part of my body that doesn't hurt." He sat in his seat on the flight deck then reached up for a control. He paused. "I can't."

"I got this." Finch intercepted and turned on the screens. "You're good." He took his pilot's seat.

Curt came from the back of the Omni. "Everything is secure," he announced. "Is Ben still complaining?"

Everyone grumbled a, "Yes."

"Man, and we gave you a couple days of rest." Curt checked the belts on Rey's chair along with Nate's. "Hope you aren't like this the whole trip." He gave a pat to Ben's back as he took his seat.

"Ow."

Curt looked back at him.

"Seriously, everything hurts. You guys weren't target practice."

Westerman leaned from his chair into the aisle. "Hey, guys, I'm really glad you let me tag along."

"No problem, son. Glad to have you," Finch told him.

Even though the tiebreak vote determined they would stay, it didn't mean they couldn't utilize the Omni. The ship was fully charged, and like Quinn and the Genesis, the crew of the Omni were going to see the earth. They would orbit the planet, landing where they could, capturing images and seeing with their own eyes the changes that had occurred.

There was a sense of peace amongst them on the decision to stay. They would do their best to make a new life. They weren't sure if they would join Quinn and the others, but if they didn't, they would keep close.

Until then, they were going to finish their original mission and explore the new earth. They would do so completely without the constraints of a two-week time limit. See each land, each sea, find civilizations of generations that had defied the odds of extinction.

It was new and exciting, dangerous and a little scary. While it was their home, it was alien to them.

Despite the survival of humankind, Earth had been cleansed, reborn and the crew of Omni-4, like the earth, had been given a fresh start.

One they would take, one step, one day, and one flight at a time.

It was time to go.

"Let's do this," Finch said as he fired up the engines.

ABOUT THE AUTHOR

Jacqueline Druga is a native of Pittsburgh, PA. Her works include genres of all types but she favours post-apocalypse and apocalypse writing.

Follow the author:

Facebook: @jacquelinedruga

Twitter: @gojake

Website: www.jacquelinedruga.com

www.vulpine-press.com

www.ingramcontent.com/pod-product-compliance
Lightning Source LLC
Chambersburg PA
CBHW031958190626
46808CB00018B/1912